Bound
Amanda K. Dudley-Penn

Other books by Amanda K. Dudley-Penn found in paperback

The Alexandra Denton Chronicles
The Hidden
The Appointed

The Brazil Werewolf Series
Beckoned

Coming Soon to paperback
Summoned (Book 2) The Brazil Werewolf Series
The Fallen (Book 3) The Alexandra Denton Chronicles

Books Available on Kindle

The Alexandra Denton Chronicles
The Hidden
The Appointed
The Fallen

The Brazil Werewolf Series
Beckoned
Summoned

The Preston Vampire Series
Bound

Coming soon to Kindle
Unbound (Book 2) The Preston Vampire Series
Enticed (Book 3) The Brazil Werewolf Series
The Sacrifice (Book 4) The Alexandra Denton Chronicles

Coming in 2015 to Kindle

Guardian (Book 1) The Angel Essence Series

Books Available on Nook

<u>The Alexandra Denton Chronicles</u>
The Hidden
The Appointed

<u>The Brazil Werewolf Series</u>
Beckoned
Summoned

<u>The Preston Vampire Series</u>
Bound

<u>Coming soon to Nook</u>
The Fallen (Book 3) The Alexandra Denton Chronicles

-

Acknowledgments

I would like to thank my beautiful daughters, Constance and Isabella and my handsome son, Joshua and my equally handsome husband, David. Thank you for standing by me during the writing of this book. Also, I would like to thank my mother, Kaye Hirjak and step-father, Paul Hirjak. I would like to thank my siblings, James Matthews, Josh Matthews, Michael Dudley, Kara Wallace and Amber Dudley. I would also like to thank my other momma, Tammy Laliberte. I would like to thank my sister-in-laws, Carolyne Graves, Roxanna Matthews, Amanda Johnson-Penn and Corie Matthews and my brother-in-laws, Carl Penn, Harold Fuller and Joe Wallace. I want to give thanks to my adopted brother, Robert Sanders and adopted brother-in-law, Alvin Craig. I would also like to thank my adopted sisters, Sandra Pressley, Chrystal Ambrose, Hopi Craig and Connie Sanchez and my aunts, Connie Sekulich, Vickie Edwards, Karen Williams, Peggy Russell-Englant, Nancy Holt, Amy Russell and Becky Dudley, Brenda Rollins, Antoinette Triolo and my uncles, Jason Russell, Anthony Russell, Terry Russell, Kenneth Matthews, David Dudley and Gary Dudley. I would also like to thank my cousins, Michelle Dudley, Josh Jordan, Valerie Russell, Rebecca Grieshaber, Brian Russell, Lisa Anderson, Traci Coble, Dena Fly, Catareena Taber, Christel Metcalf, Shae Hill, Autumn Sweeton and Buffy Russell and my Grandmother, Mildred Hardy and my grandfather, Charles Russell. I would also like to thank my friends, Melanie Simmons, Sonya Erdman, Mandiey Hill, Mendy Millner and Anna Marquez, Robert Harry, Bob Ramirez, Nikki, Cindy and Jason Fryman, Valerie Rose, Karen Kilpatrick Roberts, Brendra Kilpatrick Paul, Penny Duval, Jennifer Willis and Ann Harry. I would also like to thank my models for my upcoming books, Leanna Morris, Mckenzie Zani, Tami, Alexis McGregor, Alexis Millner, Jessica May, Lacy Bryant-Thomas, Mariah Bryant, Jesse Bryant, Christopher Thomas, Tyler Dennis Cory Laliberte and of course I would like to thank my daughters, Constance and Isabella again for being the models for this cover. I would also like to give a special thanks to my little ones teachers, Mrs. Lawson, Mrs. Cardin, Mrs. Deniz, Mrs. Ables and the aides, Mrs. Lopez and Mrs. Flores. Thank you everyone.

I dedicate this book in memory of my daddy, Eric Ray Dudley. I love you and miss you so much. I will never forget you.

Prologue

The significance of life is that all creatures have both good and evil within them. As Marissa Dalene looked into the eyes of the creature which approached her, she saw all of the contrasts of that belief. He was both man and monster…friend and enemy and someone who she both loved and hated.

She watched his gait trying to decide whether it was predatory or not as he walked closer and closer. Her heart sped up; pounding the blood through her veins in what seemed a last attempt to stay alive.

10.

She closed her eyes and swallowed over the lump in her throat as her name whispered softly to her on the breeze. Slowly, she took a deep breath and looked up into the eyes of the one who would choose her fate.

"Marissa," he said, again. She noticed that tears rested in his eyes. It was another contrast. He felt guilt for the evil deeds he had done and would still do. She swallowed as she realized that if he suffered from guilt, her fate was sealed.

Her lips trembled as a single tear fell from her eye as he reached for her in silence. He said nothing. He offered no apology. She didn't move away but sighed as he pulled her to him. She closed her eyes against the darkness as he lowered his head to her throat causing another tear to fall down her cheek. However, this tear was in mourning of a the life she would have led. This tear was the final one she would shed before she closed her eyes in death.

Chapter One
Meetings

One Year Earlier

She was entranced. It was the only excuse Marissa had for the absolute peace she experienced as she walked to the lake near her home in Winchester, Tennessee. Her mind didn't wander. Instead, she stayed focused on the impending coolness of the water in the heat of the day.

Sadly, neither the fact that her sister, Karena was ill and had been unable to join her nor that Marissa was alone and her parents would have forbidden her from going could gain importance. She did not think of the danger and even if she did, she would not have cared. She stopped only long enough to remove her sandals and the shorts and shirt that covered her bikini before stepping into the lapping waves. She smiled at the euphoria of it as she stepped further and further into the water until she was waist deep and then, fell backwards, swimming on her back as she closed her eyes. It surprised her at how close it was to meditation…to perfect serenity.

Her eyes opened and she looked up into the blue sky and breathed slowly in and out. She had been so enthralled that she hadn't expected the pain that sliced through her side with such ferocity that it ruined any sense of peace she experienced.

She kicked as she sank beneath the murky, gray-green water of the lake. Panic seized her as pain sliced through her again and again. She thrashed with the force of it, trembling as the realization that she was without help and would have to save herself slammed through her mind. There was no one there to save her and she could only blame herself. She shouldn't have come alone. She should have stayed home where she was safe.

She sank a little further as the pain subsided. She began to kick again trying to push her head above the surface believing that the danger had passed.

Her blue-green eyes stung from the dirt in the water as she tried to see the light above her. Her long strawberry blonde hair floated above her in thick water-darkened strands blocking her ability to see. She moved upwards again causing her hair to push backward enough to view the sun. She pushed further up until she broke the surface again and gasped in gulps of air before the pain returned to her side causing her to sink below the water once again. Her eyes widened as she realized that the danger was not over yet.

She kicked her legs, forcing herself to rise in the water

again but this time liquid filled her lungs and she struggled to the surface only managing a gulp of air before sinking. This time she sank further. Slowly, she opened her eyes. She tried to raise her arms but found them too heavy with fatigue, causing her to be only able to kick with her feet.

Pain slashed through her side once more and she lost what was left of the precious oxygen she had held in her lungs. Darkness took her and slowly, painfully she lost consciousness.

She didn't know how long it was before the sensation of being pulled toward the surface struck her. She tried to open her eyes but they felt as if they had been sealed shut. A few moments later, cool air hit her skin. She tried to inhale but she realized with horror that she was still drowning.

A moment later, she was lifted and put on the rough ground.
 Someone's hands pushed roughly on her chest causing the water to rise up her throat but they stopped right before it was pushed into her mouth.

Please don't stop, Marissa thought, panicked.

As if the person were listening to her thoughts, they placed their hands back on her chest. She heard a male's voice a moment later, "Breathe," he whispered, "Please breathe."

Slowly, the water rose up her throat and pooled in her mouth right before exploding from between her lips as she coughed and gagged the water from her lungs.

She seemed to cough forever before it finally stopped. Her chest burned as she gasped oxygen in through her nose and mouth. Her eyes opened and she inhaled sharply. She blinked as she looked up at the man who had saved her.

Her eyes widened at his appearance. He seemed more angel than man with light blonde hair and sky blue eyes. He had

14.
a square, masculine face with a roman nose and full lips. His body was muscular and tanned a light brown with droplets of water here and there.

"You look just like her," he whispered and then, shook his head when she frowned up at him wondering what he meant. Finally, he looked back at her with concern shining from his eyes, "Are you okay?"

She frowned as she tried to understand what he had said but he shook his head distracting her, "What's your name?" He asked with a slight accent that she could only place as European.

Marissa opened her mouth and pushed her name slowly out of her lips, "M-Marissa," she croaked over the burning of her throat.

"Marissa," he whispered and then, smiled kindly, "I'm Bernard...Bernard Talbot. I will be the one who will be taking you to the hospital."

Marissa nodded as exhaustion swamped her again. She wanted to talk. She wanted to move. She wanted to thank him but fatigue took her and she fell into the darkness once more.

****

One Month Later

Marissa felt the pounding of her feet matching the rhythm of the music vibrating through the small ear buds as she ran in the forest near her home. Her breath flowed in and out of her lungs peacefully.

She inhaled deeply as her muscles relaxed. Her morning run calmed her. It released her from all of her stress. Unfortunately, there was a lot of stress lately and it all came from one person...Bernard.

Her pace slowed as she brought his image to her mind.

She couldn't deny that he was attractive with his thick sunshine blonde hair and sky blue eyes. He truly did appear angelic. However, his celestial looks weren't enough to make her want more than friendship from him. Obviously, neither was his charm nor the fact that he had saved her life.

She slowed her pace as she contemplated her sanity. Maybe she was crazy. Her friends believed she was. Even her mother thought so. The only person in her life that seemed to understand her reluctance to date Bernard was Thalia, her godmother.

She smiled as Thalia's face rose to her mind. She was a proud African-American woman with skin the color of caramel. She was a round woman but Marissa believed she had been slender in her youth. Her hair was a beautiful mixture of black and bronze but Thalia's eyes showed her true beauty. They were the color of tanned leather and always shown with warmth and love for everyone…everyone but Bernard. Her dislike of him or anyone was a rare thing.

Marissa lost her smile. Why didn't Thalia like him? It was odd especially since she had never told her why. Thalia never kept secrets. Still, she had and Marissa found herself going through all of the scenarios in her mind.

She had been concentrating on those scenarios so much that she had not been paying attention and ran into a wall of hard chest and arms, causing her to fall backward.

She let out a breath of exasperation as she looked up into Bernard's blue eyes. He grinned as he held out his hand. She narrowed her eyes at him as she took the ear buds from her ears but finally, took his hand allowing him to pull her up.

"What are you doing here?" She asked, frowning. She noticed that he did not stepped away from her. Instead, he rested

16.

his hands on her waist. She sighed knowing she couldn't step away without hurting his feelings.

He raised one thick brow, "Well, I was looking for you," he said and shrugged, "Your mother told me you were here."

Annoyance crept up her spine. Why couldn't her mother stay out of this? It was irritating, "And you got here before me?"

He grinned, "It is not my fault if you are extremely slow, Marissa."

She couldn't keep the smile from crossing her face, "I'm not slow," she said, and then, shook her head, "However, it does worry me that a strange man is waiting for me in the forest."

He rolled his eyes, "I'm not strange," he said as his eyes darkened. He studied her face carefully, "I'm your friend…or at least I thought I was before you began to avoid me."

Marissa shifted, uncomfortably, "You are my friend," she said softly. She looked up at him as her heart sank. She couldn't keep the truth from him any longer and when she spoke her voice trembled, "Only I think you want more."

He frowned as his eyes darkened further. He swallowed visibly and then, closed them blocking her out. When he opened them again the pain was clearly there, "And you don't?"

She shifted again, "You're my friend," she whispered.

He pressed his lips together and nodded once before looking back at her," And that's it?" He asked, turning from her. She watched as his shoulders trembled. Guilt shot through her, "That's all you want from me?"

Seconds ticked by before she could answer. Finally, she whispered, "Yes…For now at least."

She watched him nod and then, he turned back to her with tears resting in his eyes, "I love you," he said and held up his hand when she opened her mouth to protest, "But if you need time…and all I can be is your friend right now…Then, I'll be just your friend."

She swallowed, seeing the pain clear on his face. Marissa"s head fell causing her chin to fall toward her chest. She wanted to fix this even if she was the one who had smashed his heart into. Slowly, she stepped forward and hugged him. He kissed the top of her head.

"Thank you," she whispered.

He wrapped his arms around her, "No thanks needed," he said in a thick voice.

She looked up at him, trying to make him see that she did care but he backed away. Her heart clenched again and the need to fix him hit her once more.

"Are you still coming with me to the fireworks?" She asked, forcing herself to look into his face.

He swallowed visibly, "No, Marissa," he said in an emotion thick voice, "I think I need a little time."

She nodded as her heart sank. He stepped in front of her and gently placed a kiss on her forehead. "I'll see you later, okay?" He asked, reaching up and caressing her cheek. She nodded her head.

"Of course you will," she whispered.

He nodded again. Then, he turned and walked away leaving Marissa staring after him with regret ripping through her soul.

****

Nicolas Preston walked into the park in Winchester, Tennessee on the Fourth of July experiencing a thrill that he had not felt in a long time. Maybe it was because he had finally come home after a century away…or perhaps it was because of the fireworks. Either way, he became nearly euphoric as he walked toward the lake where many of the spectators gathered.

The euphoria ended a moment later at the first glance of a girl of about eighteen who sat on a checkered blanket near the lake. A tremble worked through him as he blinked repeatedly, hoping that he was mistaken…that who he viewed before him was a vision or a trick of the light.

He inhaled sharply and closed his eyes, blocking the girl from his sight while trying to convince himself he was wrong and knowing if he wasn't, he risked his sanity. He risked his soul.

Slowly, he opened his eyes, finding the girl still in front of him. He stepped closer as he observed her entranced but not because of her beauty. Instead, it was because of who she looked like that caught his undying attention…Giselle.

Red hot anger burst through him at the thought of the girl who used his love and turned it into something dark and ugly. She had punished him for every tender notion he possessed by having her true lover turn not only him but his brother and sister-in-law into monsters for the rest of their existence.

He shook with the memory of her as his whole body convulsed causing him to force his feet to stay immobile. He could not attack her within a crowd full of people. He would not put his family at risk. Still, he took another step toward her, staying far enough away from where she sat to remain unnoticed.

Hate and guilt swamped him as he continued to scrutinize every movement she made looking for any differences but finding none. He should have turned and left but he didn't and it was a mistake because when she opened her mouth to speak, he heard the same voice that had left Giselle's lips.

That fact nearly pushed him to move toward her and drain every ounce of her blood. Still, he forced himself not to move as he watched her strawberry blonde hair brush across her pale round cheek. Thankfully, he had not moved.

He studied everything about her, nearly convinced she was Giselle but desperately looking for differences. She possessed the same straight proud grace as Giselle. Her hair waved just the same. Her mouth pouted as Giselle's had. Even the small waist and height were the same. He almost attacked but she turned and he saw her eyes. They stopped him. They soothed the angry vengeful spirit which invaded his usually calm demeanor.

Her eyes shown with the same blue-green color as Giselle's had. They were so similar except for the emotion in them. They were beautiful and iridescent but lacked the coldness.

His eyes widened as she smiled at the older woman beside her. Love emanated from her…Love. Giselle had not been capable of that emotion.

All thoughts of revenge disappeared to be replaced by a familiar heart pounding emotion that he had promised himself to never experience again. It happened so quickly that he became drunk on the swift change from hate to love. In that moment, it seemed as if destiny guided him to see her. He was fated to be by her side.

He shook his head of the thought, knowing how dangerous it was. Still, he stared at her as the obsession grew. He noticed the care with which she treated the lady beside her and realized she must be her mother. Everything about this girl seemed selfless and kind. None of those things described Giselle.

He frowned as he swallowed over the lump in his throat. A change occurred that separated this girl from who he believed her to be. He blinked no longer able to see who she looked like but who she actually was. She was someone who held kindness and love…A mortal…not a vampire but brilliant and pulsing with vitality.

20.

He couldn't take his eyes off of her as she gazed at the fireworks exploding above her. He swallowed hard as he watched her beautiful face light with joy.

Slowly, her gaze lowered and nearly turned to him. He held his breath as she began to face him. It excited him that she would notice him.

"Marissa, look!" Her mother said, stopping her from meeting his gaze. Once again, she turned to the fireworks.

"Marissa," He whispered as little bursts of pleasure caused his heart to race from just allowing her name to slip past his lips.

Still, pain came a moment later as he realized that he could never see her again. He would not subject her to the eternity of darkness he suffered. He would not take away the radiance that glowed from her skin. Slowly, he backed away, knowing she would never join him. She would never be a vampire.

****

Three Months Later

Marissa slipped blissfully into sleep. It hadn't always been that way because at one time, sleep tortured her. For almost a month after her near drowning, her dreams were filled with nightmares full of fangs and blood enough to fill rivers. They had been dreams that made her scream out at the terror and frightened her to the point that the very thought of closing her eyes made her tremble. Then, he came, taking over her dreams and making them wonderful.

She did not know his name at first. She had only seen his eyes. They were beautiful and the color of bronze with long, thick lashes. In those first nights, she would stare into them feeling mesmerized and for the first time in a long while, safe within her slumber.

Then, she began to see him fully. She never knew a man to be beautiful but he was. He was tall and when she embraced him, he could rest his chin upon her head. He possessed dark hair, thick and wavy and wore it a bit long but barely touching the collar of his shirt. He had a square and masculine face with a little of the roundness in his cheeks left from his boyhood, making her guess his age at a little over her eighteen years. He had a straight and strong nose and his lips were beautifully shaped and full. He was muscular as if he worked hard labor but carried the air of a businessman. However, her favorite parts of him were his dimples which dipped into his cheeks when he spoke and when he smiled.

Then, she discovered his name and even in her waking hours, she would find herself whispering it…Nicolas. His very name spoke to her heart and soul and as she slipped into the darkness of sleep, she whispered it again.

"I'm here," she heard him say and she slowly opened her eyes to behold his handsome face.

She smiled and he caressed her face gently before kissing her with such passion that her heart trembled. She held him not wanting to let go but knowing she would have to. It wasn't natural to be in love with a dream.

He pulled away from her and looked down into her face, "I will love you forever."

"I will always love you too," she said, experiencing a bout of panic as she said the next words, "Even when I have to let you go."

Nicolas' face fell as he caressed her cheek, "You will see me soon, Marissa. I swear it."

She nodded though she didn't believe him. She wouldn't lose that final grip on reality.

22.

He leaned down and kissed her again and she couldn't help but to return his passion. As he kissed her, the dream faded leaving complete emptiness in her heart. She found herself sobbing as her eyes opened to light spilling through the windows of her room. Still, she lay there allowing her tears to fall upon her pillows for a man she had never truly met.

She fought a sob as she sunk deeper into what she only knew as insanity because she was in love, but only with a dream.

****

Nicolas stood peering out of the living room window of his home as a deep sadness settled into his soul. The trees that surrounded the property stood tall but not so tall as to cover the view of the mountains in the distance. He saw the trees swaying in the wind as the sun rose above the range and cast a bright halo of orange light upon them. It was breathtaking but still a shudder worked through him. He couldn't concentrate on the beauty. Instead, he recalled the last words that Marissa had said within their dreams.

I will always love you too, even when I have to let you go, she had said.

His heart had broken when she spoke those words. He loved her. He no longer denied that fact though he had tried three months earlier to do just that. He had almost convinced himself that his infatuation with her was due only to her resemblance to Giselle but then the dreams began.

He didn't ask for them and had been truly distraught until he spoke to his sister-in-law, Elizabeth. She understood and although Nicolas had put her and his brother, Frazier in danger before for love, she encouraged his feelings. She had even insisted they purchase the property neighboring the Dalene property. They had moved in a week before and the closeness only heightened the bond between him and Marissa. He could almost sense every breath she took.

As he stood at the window, he had to fight the impulse to go to her. He couldn't bear the thought of her with someone else. He turned and walked to one of the chairs Elizabeth had placed near the fireplace and sank into it. He rubbed one course hand down his face.

"You should feed, Nick," a deep voice said.

He looked up to find his brother, Frazier standing in front of him. Nicolas studied him silently. He was a handsome man and at least two inches taller than Nicolas' six feet. His hair was dark brown but so dark it was nearly black. His face was square and strong with deep emerald eyes peering from it. His nose was long and thin and his lips were very full. Although he was tall, he was not considered lanky but leanly muscled and there seemed to be a gracefulness to him that most tall men did not have. He always dressed expensively. Even as Nicolas looked at him, he saw that his business suit was tailored to fit him perfectly.

"You're thinking of her again," Frazier said and Nicolas only nodded his head to affirm it.

Frazier sighed heavily as he sat in the matching chair across from him. He seemed worried. Nicolas winced as guilt twisted in his gut.

"I love her," Nicolas said, trying to make Frazier understand but voicing it sounded insane even to him when he had never met her.

"I know," Frazier said, smiling sadly, "I've known for a while."

Nicolas raised his brows in surprise," You have?"

"It was obvious," Frazier said with a shrug.

Nicolas nodded, "I'm sorry. I know that this puts

everyone in danger."

Frazier tilted his head, "I'm not angry at you for being in love, Nick. I understand."

Nicolas frowned as he gazed into his brother's face. The strain was evident, "If you're not upset that I love her…then, why are you upset?" Nicolas asked cautiously.

Frasier rubbed his bottom lip nervously with the tips of his fingers and glanced away for a moment. When he met Nicolas' eyes again, there was a new determination there.

He took a deep breath and began to speak very slowly, "Since your infatuation with Marissa began, we have been gleaning information from the town about her and her family," he said as Nicolas narrowed his eyes. Frasier raised his hand in defense, "It wasn't with evil intent. We just wanted to know more about her."

"You still shouldn't have done it," Nicolas said, relaxing.

"Maybe not but I wouldn't judge that until after you hear what we learned," He said, looking away for a moment.

It was then that Nicolas noticed that Elizabeth entered the room. As always, she reminded Nicolas of a porcelain doll with her pale skin and long black hair that twisted in massive curls down her back. She possessed large innocent blue eyes peering from a delicate heart shaped face. A light blue silk dress draped her tiny frame and she wore light blue sandals on her small pedicured feet.

"What did you learn?" Nicolas asked with an odd sense of fright.

"Well, history does repeat itself," Elizabeth said in her wonderfully musical voice that rarely seemed to match any mood but
happiness. Still, he knew the next words would be ominous, "Bernard is here."

Anger pierced Nicolas as the name of the vampire who changed them and took Giselle was repeated in his head but then, terror shook him as Elizabeth spoke again.

"And it seems that he is a friend of Marissa's," she said, softly.

Nicolas began to shake with anger," What does he want with her?" He asked, "He has Giselle."

"We can only believe that he means to change her or kill her," Frazier said, swallowing before saying the next words, "Of course, that depends upon whether Giselle still walks the earth or not. Either way we'll have to protect Marissa."

Nicolas tried to calm himself as he looked at Elizabeth and Frazier, "Then, I must go to her soon," he said, "We must make . sure that I am introduced to Marissa formally."

Both Frazier and Elizabeth nodded their heads, giving their blessings. However, instead of relief that his family approved, Nicolas only felt terror because he knew their reasons.

Chapter Two
Reality

Marissa was not able to go back to sleep. Instead, she found herself standing on the wooden balcony just outside her room which gave a beautiful view of her family's property. She watched the sun rise turning the trees surrounding the property from silhouettes into the bright green of leaves and pine needles and the deep brown of the trunks. A stream cut through the trees bordering the property which bubbled with waters that her grandmother swore could heal any illness.

Usually, this scene calmed her. She loved her home but as she looked out over the beautiful scene, the emotions she experienced were anything but peaceful. Instead, she was confused and frightened all because of one insistant sentiment that would not go away. There was a strong sense of nearness with Nicolas. It was overwhelming and she couldn't shake it no matter what she did. Sadly, it wasn't the first time she had experienced this feeling. It was beginning to become a familiar occurance.

She sighed, as the uneasiness crept further into her mind. She would have to do something soon. Her family and friends were already beginning to question her strange behavior. They thought there was something wrong because she wasn't dating. Worse, she wasn't even interested. If they knew the truth, they'd really think she was crazy. If they knew that she loved a dream, they'd probably have her committed.

She blinked back tears, knowing she needed to be strong and pushed thoughts of Nicolas away. Slowly, her mind drifted as it always did to Bernard. Her mother would be happy if she chose him. Also, Bernard would be happy. If she was honest with herself she would have to admit that he may be the closest option to love for her.

Still, when she tried to imagine dating him, her stomach turned. It shouldn't be so troubling. She should want to date him. He was handsome, rich and charming but most importantly he was real. Her heart clinched in her chest, knowing that none of those reasons mattered. She loved Nicolas and she wouldn't use Bernard because regardless of anything else, she did care for him.

"Marissa!" She heard Thalia call from her room, shattering her thoughts. Her head snapped up and her eyes widened as she realized that it was much later than she had originally thought. Her shoulders drooped forward as she realized she would not be able to go for her morning run. It was too late and she was supposed to help Thalia shop for her daughter, Eliza's birthday party.

She winced realizing how much she had forgotten, "I'm out here," she called, seeing Thalia step through the door a moment later.

With the first glimpse of Thalia's face, Marissa noticed that her mood was thunderous. She tilted her head studying the woman who had always been more like a second mother to her than a neighbor or a babysitter. After all, when Marissa's mother had returned to work, Thalia had been the one to care for her and Karena.

However as Thalia progressed toward her, she did not see the woman who had gently rocked her to sleep. Instead, she saw a woman who seemed angry and fearful.

"Thalia, are you alright?" Marissa asked, cautiously.

"No," she whispered, looking up at Marissa with a steadily darkening face, "I won't be taking you with me to go shopping."

Marissa frowned, trying to understand if she had done something to make Thalia mad, "Why not?"

"Your mother has agreed to a visit from Bernard," she said, spitting his name as her eyes narrowed and her nose flared. Her teeth clenched so tightly that the muscles of her jaw showed in stark relief.

Marissa groaned, "Why did she do that?" She asked, rolling her eyes, "Does she like seeing him leave with his feelings hurt?"

"No, she's hoping you'll change your mind and date him," Thalia said, as her eyes widened fearfully.

"Well, I'm not going to change my mind," Marissa said, turning and walking into her room, "I don't have those types of feelings for him."

Thalia's face relaxed in relief and the anger began to fade from her face, "Well, I'm glad for that."

Marissa frowned, "You don't like him much do you, Thalia?"

Thalia shook her head, "No, I don't."

Marissa nodded, not asking why because she could already tell that Thalia wouldn't tell her, "Well then, I suppose you won't be mad at me for not dating him."

Thalia shook her head, "No, I won't ever be angry at you

for that."

Marissa smiled relieved. At least Thalia wouldn't be pushing her toward him in hopes that she would date him. She sighed, knowing that she would probably be the only one.

****

Bernard Talbot looked out of the window in the living room of Marissa's home as he waited for her to arrive. He wasn't really looking at anything beyond the glass. Instead, he was trying to make sense of all of the thoughts swirling throughout his mind. Truthfully, he felt as if he were slowly going crazy. After all he had been tortured for months and it was not about to end any time soon.

One subject of his torture was near. Marissa's energy floated softly in the air as she walked toward the room. He stiffened knowing that she didn't suspect the darkness around her…darkness he did not
want to touch her. Still, it *would* touch her because his hand was being forced.

His mother had given her orders and no one denied her without serious consequences. He had learned that lesson well. Those consequences were too great to ignore and would require more than just his life. Still, he would try to find a way to save Marissa even though he realized that time was running out. When that happened, there would be absolutely nothing he could do.

He inhaled as her energy grew. Her scent swirled around him and he heard her very close but he didn't turn to her. Instead, he continued to gaze out of the window, hoping to wipe the guilt and unrest from his face. So, he concentrated on a tree in the forest, hoping to give the appearance of studying something very far away.

30.

"Do you see something, Bernard?" She asked in that sweet voice, tinged in a Southern accent. He pretended to jump as if she had startled him, causing her to place her hand apologetically on his shoulder.

"No nothing," he said, managing a wide grin, "I was just admiring your family's property."

She pursed her lips and for a moment he studied her face. As always, he tried to search for differences in the appearances of Marissa and Giselle. As usual he found none. He swallowed hard as he admitted how frightened he was that someone could resemble someone else so much but even as he looked at her, he recognized it was more than that. Marissa shared more than looks with Giselle. She shared some of her prefrences including the way she dressed and even some of her manurisms. It was…eerie.

"It is beautiful, isn't it?" Marissa asked, looking out of the window for an instant. She had only glanced but a look of longing crossed her face for a reason he did not understand. For a moment, he fought the temptation to read her mind and won. He would not commit that invasion.

"Marissa, I guess you are wondering about my visit," he finally said and then, sighed. She tilted her head as she studied him causing him to shift uncomfortably. He swallowed before he spoke, "The truth is I'm worried about our friendship. I understand that you worry about my…feelings for you but I promise I would never act on them if you didn't want me to."

He watched as her face softened and heartbreak shined clear in her eyes, "I know you would never act on your feelings and it makes me sad to think that you are so worried," she said and then, sighed, "Bernard, you will always be my friend."

He should have guarded himself against those words but

he didn't and a sudden desperation took him, "Do you promise that?"

She frowned as she parted her lips to answer but a knock sounded at the door. They turned toward it finding Thalia standing with her mouth opened in shock. She began to tremble when she met Bernard's gaze. He frowned as his eyes held hers realizing her fear.

He pursed his lips as he studied her, wondering why she seemed so frightened. He went over everything he remembered of her in his mind. Her name was Thalia Sorenson and she had once been Marissa's babysitter. She was also her godmother. As far as he recalled, he had only saw her at a distance. He had never even spoken to her. She couldn't possibly recognize who or what he was. Still, that did not explain why she seemed afraid of him.

She took an unconscious step backwards and that movement stirred the air around her. Bernard inhaled sharply as the earthy scent of the woman invaded his senses. In an instant, a memory came to him so sharply that he blanched. Thalia did know him. He had harmed her once. Worse, she did know what he was.

"Bernard, are you alright?" Marissa asked. Concern laced her voice.

He turned to her, forcing a smile, "Yes," he said but his voice was weak, "But I think it's time for me to go."

Marissa frowned as she studied his face, "Okay," she said, slowly, "Are you sure you are alright?"

"Yes," he said, knowing that he must look ill, "I will see you later?"

Marissa smiled, though she was obviously still concerned as she nodded, "Of course."

32.

He smiled and then, turned and walked to the door. Thalia backed up as he stood in front of her, nearly hitting her back on the doorframe. He closed his eyes as his suspicions were confirmed. He swallowed hard as he walked past her quickly, knowing he would have to face her…knowing he would have to prevent her from telling Marissa what he truly was.

****

Thalia rushed across the street from the Dalene's home to her own house after her encounter with Bernard Talabot. Though Marissa had begun to question her about why she reacted with so much fear to Bernard, she had not answered any of her questions. Instead, she left Marissa confused and frustrated. Guilt plagued Thalia but she couldn't tell her the truth. Marissa would think she was crazy.

Her hands shook as she opened the door to her house, quickly locking the door and walked into the living room exuding a breath of relief. For a moment, she stood in the middle of the living room unable to move. Her legs shook violently. She closed her eyes and swallowed as images of a past that she tried to forget came before her. Colors and growls and screams assaulted her and she feared that she might see these images every time she slumbered. She forced her eyes open pushing the images away.

The air seemed thick and for a long while, she stood with her mouth opened trying to force air through her mouth and nose and into her lungs. Her heart seemed to have outgrown her chest. With each pound, it threatened to break free of her ribs.

Finally, she was able to take a deep breath and walk to the window. Fear made her stomach quake and another tremor shook her. She closed her eyes, hoping that she would recover, but she knew that she wouldn't. She never would. The only thing she would willingly permit her mind to ponder on was the girl she had watched over as if she were her own.

"God, please help me to protect Marissa," she whispered as a tear fell down her cheek. Pure terror enveloped her at the idea of the danger that Marissa was in.

"You didn't say a prayer for yourself," she heard the voice from her nightmares say. She stiffened as he stepped closer to her, "Are you really that selfless?"

Slowly, she turned to face Bernard who was leaning against the doorframe to the living room. She trembled. She had been sure that she locked the door but for a monster like Bernard she was sure that a locked door did not matter.

"Why can't you leave me alone?" She asked with her voice small and more than a little panicked.

Bernard laughed, cruelly, "Maybe it's because you know something that I do not want you to tell Marissa," he sneered, "You know *what* I am."

Thalia felt a sudden burst of anger overriding her fear, "She wouldn't believe me if I told her," Her voice lowered as she shook her head, "She'd think I'd gone crazy!"

He cocked an eyebrow at her, "Still, she respects you and your opinion of me may alter hers."

Thalia narrowed her eyes at him, "Why did you choose her?" Thalia asked, feeling her heart pounding harder with each beat, "Why couldn't you have chosen someone else?"

For a moment, Bernard's face softened and it looked as if guilt clouded his features. Thalia frowned. She could not have believed that a monster such as Bernard was able to experience guilt. Still, if there was guilt that meant that he was planning to hurt Marissa.

34.

"Are you going to hurt her?" Thalia asked as another Tremor shook her,"She's good. She's never done anything to you."

Bernard's face hardened and the cruel smile returned, "So was your boy," he said. Thalia noticed that he hadn't answered her question. Instead, he had decided to bring up the most painful memory that she had. He looked at her quizzically, "Do you ever wonder what happened to him?"

"You've killed him. That's what happened to him," she cried unable to hold in her grief, "It's cruel to make me hope for anything else."

She had spoken too loud and she saw the panic settle on Bernard's face as he glanced over his shoulder, sniffing the air as he did. Then, it seemed as if he disappeared but a second later, he reappeared in front of her. A cry escaped her as she realized that he was only an inch from her face.

He put his finger to her lips, "Shhh," he said and she instantly quieted because in her mind, she realized he was too close and he would kill her before anyone would be able to save her. She also realized anyone who tried to save her life would die and she didn't want that.

He raised his brow and spoke slowly, menacingly into her ear, "Your opinions of me are bad ones, but I do not intend on harming you," he said, inhaling very deeply, "Even if your skin smells like the earth…mouthwatering, really. Still, my intentions toward you may change if you continue to stand in my way. I may give into that very tempting thirst."

"I won't allow you to hurt her,' she said with her heart pounding even harder and faster than before.

Bernard laughed and then raised a skeptical brow, "You are going to stop me?" Bernard asked, shaking his head, "You couldn't protect your son. What makes you think that you could protect her if I *wanted* to harm her?"

"I would give my life to protect her," Thalia raised her chin.

"Then, you would be giving up your life in vain," he said, shaking his head as if amused.

"Then, I will willingly do that if it keeps her from you even if for only one moment," he leaned closer and she closed her eyes. Bile rose in her throat as the knowledge of what he intended to do entered her mind and her soul, invading them until nothing else was thought of or felt.

"I suppose you will," he said in a growl. He meant to terrify her into submission. Thalia was terrified but she wouldn't allow him to harm Marissa. Even if it meant giving her life.

She kept her eyes closed, waiting for him to strike. Fear invaded every part of her body. The heat of his breath touched her skin as her heart thundered so loud it was deafening but suddenly, he backed away, releasing her.

"Mom, are you alright?" Her daughter, Eliza's voice drifted to her only a moment later. Slowly, she opened her eyes and looked around. Bernard was gone. Eliza's arrival had saved her.

Thalia suppressed a shiver as she looked into her daughter's eyes, "Yes, I am," she said, exhaling in a rush. She swallowed hard and then, looked at her daughter who looked so much like her but at the moment, she had become her angel because she had given her more time to warn Marissa about Bernard.

****

Abigail Dubois looked down at the latest letter from her

best friend, Elizabeth Preston. Her beautiful sea green eyes brightened more and more with the look of concentration on her pretty, round face. Slowly, everything before her changed and she saw herself within a vision she would have been murdered for in her mortal life. After all, she had nearly died for a similar vision.

Before becoming a vampire, she had almost been burned at the stake for her visions. The townsfolk said that she practiced witchcraft and worshipped the devil. After she changed, her visions had only gotten stronger but never so strong as the vision before her.

In this vision, she saw herself which was rare. Her hair flowed in golden curls down her back. Her face was round with long thinly arched brows. She had a short buttoned nose and very full lips. She wasn't small like Elizabeth. As a matter of fact, she may be considered a large woman but she had rounded hips and a large bosom that made most men drop to their knees in admiration.

She moved her eyes from the study of her own face and glanced around. A battle raged around her. Two clans of vampires clashed against each other. She frowned as she tried to recognize them. She squinted into the crowd, trying to focus. Finally, she could view the vampires in the very front of the battle. Elizabeth and her husband, Frazier fought beside her husband Anrique. Abigail pushed her mind even further and found the focus of this vision. Nicolas Preston was bound and bloody. The war had something to do with him, but the vision began to fade. Only one small picture was left and that was of their greatest enemy, Lilith, lying in a pool of blood and turning to ash.

Abigail shook her head as she pulled from the vision. She

was sure of two things. Nicolas was alive at the end of the vision and Lilith would die.

Her husband, Anrique, put his arms around her, pulling her from her thoughts. She did not know how long he had been there. Still, she welcomed his comfort.

"Please say that you dreamed something good and not evil," he said and she felt her heart squeeze. She wished that she could say that fully, but she wasn't sure how many deaths would ensue for the one that would free them all.

She shook her head, "We must go to America. We must go to Elizabeth," she said, grasping onto the one hope within the vision, "There Lilith will meet her end."

Anrique looked at her as understanding dawned, "A war?"

She nodded her head, "Gather the families," she said, raising her chin, "I will go to Elizabeth and her family and prepare them. You will meet me there after informing the rest of the families."

He nodded once, not bothering to argue. The war would mean peace for their kind. His eyes darkened with determination and he kissed her lips before turning around to make the arrangements for his departure. She swallowed hard, knowing that for the first time, she would have to leave without her husband and deliver news that may not be well accepted.

Chapter Three
Hope and Promises of War

Nicolas stood within the shadows of Bernard Talbot's property. It loomed over him like a ghost within the black night. Still, he wouldn't let his gaze linger on the massive structure. He came for one thing and he wouldn't leave until he got it.

He hadn't told Elizabeth or Frazier where he was going. They either assumed that he was feeding or had gone for a walk. He preferred it that way. If they'd known what he planned to do, they would have tried to stop him and he couldn't allow that. He needed to protect Marissa.

He looked left and then, right before running to the nearby barn. No one saw him…which was surprising. Most vampires stayed on guard. Still, one single vampire was coming toward him.

It felt like hours before the barn doors opened and someone entered. Nicolas focused on that vampire. With the first inhale of her scent, he determined Marissa's chosen fate. Giselle was alive and standing within that very barn with her ear cocked to one side, listening. She had sensed an intruder upon entering. Slowly, she inhaled and turned toward him, though she didn't see him because he was hidden behind a massive beam.

Her steps echoed against the wooden planks as she walked to the middle of the barn. She inhaled softly and then, sighed..

"Nicolas, I know that you are here," she said seductively, "What is it you want?"

He stepped out into the light, studying her. She looked exactly as Marissa, except for her eyes. They seemed colder and without love or compassion.

"I know you heard me," She said, studying him "But I'll ask again anyway. What do you want Nicolas?"

She didn't seem a bit afraid, though she should be. After all, he was her enemy.

"Your head would be nice," he said, barely able to control his anger as he stepped further away from the beam.

She scoffed, "If that were the case, you would have already tried to take it," she said, smiling confidently, "So, what is your real reason?"

"Marissa Dalene," he said, taking a step closer, "She's why I'm here."

She touched her face and for a moment, sadness seemed to

cloud her eyes, but the look faded as soon as it had come, making him wonder if he imagined it, "You have found my likeness," she said but something did not sound right about her voice. It sounded forlorn.

"What do you plan to do with her?" He demanded, still confused.

She looked around the barn and sighed finally, looking into his eyes, "What concern is she to you?" Again that sadness laced her words and he frowned.

Nicolas stumbled over the answers in his head and finally said, "She's innocent," and even to him it sounded like it was only an excuse.

Giselle laughed then, becoming the cold woman that he had known three centuries before, "You believe that you are in love with her," she laughed and then, met his eyes with cruelty shining clear within them, "Or have you just found another version of me?"

"She's nothing like you," Nicolas said, angry at himself and angry at her laughter, "She's better than you."

Her laughter stopped abruptly and jealousy colored the tone of her voice, "Really?" She asked with her voice dripping with venom, "Perhaps, we shall see who is better when she is dead."

Quicker than any human could perceive, Nicolas moved in front of her grasping her by the neck.

"If you harm her, Giselle, I *will* kill you," he growled and then, released her as quickly as he grabbed her and was already back within the shadows of the night.

Behind him, Giselle continued to scream, not in fear or because he hurt her but in anger and jealousy. With that scream, he knew what he had come to find out. He had to protect Marissa because Bernard was going to kill her.

****

Bernard narrowed his eyes as he wiped his mouth on his hands and then, looked at himself in the reflection of the creek he stood over. It bubbled merrily not matching the picture that reflected on its surface…the picture of a monster.

He frowned as a shudder traveled from his head to his feet so violently that he wondered for a moment if he would fall. Every time he tasted human blood, his body reacted with this much intensity.. Heaven and hell had mixed, leaving him euphoric and suffering at the same time. Within those moments, he struggled to keep tight control of the want of blood.

Finally, the lust faded and only vitality pulsed through his veins. Slowly, he turned back to the man who gave his blood. Tears burned in his bright blue eyes and it turned Bernard's stomach, sickening him.

"Don't worry," Bernard said to the man pushing his thoughts into his mind, "No more harm will come to you."

He didn't need to calm the man's fear. After all, he would forget Bernard within minutes. However, he had done the man enough cruelties and the one kind act he could do was to calm his fears sooner.

It seemed to take hours before the man's sobs quieted, but only seconds passed. Finally, the man's expression became emotionless.

Bernard studied him for a moment. He was young, perhaps eighteen, strong. His hair shined black as oil and his skin was tanned from many days working in the sun, making his eyes seem brighter. Bernard's stomach twisted again in remorse.

He swallowed and began to push his thoughts and words into the young man's mind, "You shouldn't be afraid," he said, softly, "You will not remember anything that has happened. You will not notice my bite and if anyone else notices, tell them an animal attacked you in the woods. Do not return here…ever. Now get up and go home. When you wake up, everything will be as it was this morning."

The man immediately got up and walked away. Bernard watched him until he walked out of sight and then, turned to the water, washing the blood from his hands and off of his mouth. He looked in the reflection and grimaced. The face he looked into was that of a monster but the reflection lied.

Never once had he killed and only once had he let his temper rule his behavior. He had taken Giselle and then, he changed the ones who were in his way. Even though the guilt was torture, he found comfort about one thing. They would at least be able to exist. He closed his eyes as the guilt of the encounter with the Prestons shot through him.

The guilt was a human emotion but he still clung to it. He had never wanted to be a monster but he would be soon if he couldn't find a way to save Marissa before it was too late and there would be no way back to his former self like there had been after changing the Prestons.

"My son," A siren's voice came to him. Still, he didn't turn. He knew that she was there before she spoke. As soon as he sensed her presence, he guarded his mind.

"So, you are still angry with me?" She said, but still he neither spoke nor turned. She would hate that. She believed that she deserved to be revered, worshipped and feared. After all, she was the first vampire. She was Lilith.

"You must see that I do everything for your own good," she said, losing her patience, "You mustn't hold onto mortality. You're stronger than them. They are mere food. You are a vampire. You are immortal. You should *want* to crush them."

"I was mortal once," he said, finally turning to her.

He should have caught his breath at the first sight of her but he didn't. Most would. She was alluring and beautiful. Gold, red and brown strands made up the color of her hair. Her skin was smooth and pale. All of these things usually drew mortals to her, like flies to the spider. However, when close enough they would see her eyes. They were unearthly, turning blue, green, grey and brown within seconds. Then, they would want to scream in terror but it would be too late. She would have already drained them before they opened their mouths.

She looked at him, curiously, "Maybe I *should* have crushed you," she said, sneering, "You have been nothing but a disappointment."

"You're crushing me now," he said, angry," You have done the cruelest thing possible."

She smiled in a way that showed just how cruel she could be, "You shouldn't disappoint me," she said, flashing her long canines, "Besides, I haven't done anything...*yet* but I will if you do not do as I've asked."

Bernard narrowed his eyes, "Why are you here? Is it to torment me further?" he asked as his anger rose, but he couldn't think of saving Marissa while she stood within the same vicinity as he did. She would read it within his mind and his suffering would become worse as would Marissa's.

"Actually, I thought that you would like to know that your wife was attacked in the barn," she said, smiling smugly.

Bernard's eyes widened as panic hit him square in his chest. His mother hated Giselle and would not have come unless something horrible had happened.

"Don't look so panicked," she said, laughing, "She's

unharmed…unfortunately. The problem is *who* attacked her. He's one of the ones that you changed."

Fear trembled through him. The only ones that he had changed were the Prestons and it didn't take him long to figure out who had attacked Giselle.

"Nicolas?" He asked, hoping that he was wrong.

"Yes," Lilith said, confirming his worst fears, "It seems that he's taken an interest in Marissa. This complicates things doesn't it?" She patted his cheek with one pale hand, "But you'll work through it, won't you?"

She laughed as she turned, leaving him ready to scream in utter hopelessness. Tears coursed down his face as he felt pain like no other.

Then, she disappeared and he found himself alone with his pain, but somewhere in the darkness, he heard a voice that sounded like a ray of light.

"Don't worry, Bernard," the voice of a female said, "Help is coming and we will save what is left of your mortality."

Bernard looked up as a tremble shook him to his core. She was a vampire unknown to him, but offering him hope and her voice offered him his soul. He would not ignore it.

"Come to me soon," he whispered, "I don't have much time."

A moment later the answer came and peace settled over him for the first time in his long life, "I will," the voice answered.

****

Elizabeth sensed the intruder before actually seeing her. She sat up in bed as a tremor of knowing slid through her. Her fangs sharpened, ready for an attack.

She ran her tongue over her teeth as she looked beside her, finding Frazier gone. She sent her mind out in search of him and found him on the other side of the property. She inhaled again and found Nicolas closer. He was just entering the borders of the tree line around the house. She closed her eyes focusing harder on him.

Someone is here, she projected to him.

The answer came a moment later, *I'm on my way.*

She didn't answer him back. He knew that she would be careful. She inhaled again, finding the scent of a vampiress. Then, she began to get a picture of her. She saw her flashing sea green eyes and golden curls. She smiled as she walked to the door and threw it open.

"Abigail," she whispered, confused. What was she doing in Winchester? The last she had heard, she was in Paris, France.

"Don't look so frightened, Elizabeth," she said, raising one long, thin brow, "I'm not going to eat you. Friends…even very good ones don't quench my thirst."

Elizabeth stared at her in shock and a little bit of jealousy. As always, Abigail was breathtaking, but the jealousy faded too quickly to cause any spite at all. Instead, she felt a deep friendship. She went to her and embraced her.

Elizabeth released her looking around for Abigail's husband. Never had Elizabeth seen her without him, but she found that he wasn't near nor did she sense him.

"Where's Anrique?" She asked, frowning as she looked back at her.

Abigail's grin faded and she looked a bit guilty, "He's retrieving the family…to bring them here."

Elizabeth swallowed as fear leapt into her chest. The only time that the family was together was for war.

"A war?" Elizabeth asked, twisting her hands frantically in front of her.

46.

Abigail nodded her head, "But don't be so frightened, Elizabeth," she said, softly, "This war ends in Lilith's death."

Chapter Four
Bloodlines and Meetings

The vampiress who had spoken to Bernard stood within the shadows of the trees surrounding the Talbot property with her eyes narrowed. She searched out with her mind and found Lilith nowhere near. Tentatively, she stepped forward. Anger burned within her sky blue eyes and the wind whipped her long wheat blonde hair, making her seem like an angry spectre, instead of the vampire she was.

She studied the house where Bernard lived. It loomed

large and white with two stories. It was squared in the front and round in the back. The porch stretched around the bottom level. The windows were tall and narrow and evenly spaced along each floor. It seemed beautiful and innocent but she knew the evil that resided there and that knowledge marred the home's appearance in her eyes.

She looked up at the second floor of the home, letting her senses find Lilith's room and smiled. Revenge was going to be so sweet and long overdue. She would need only to be patient for a little while longer.

Her eyes narrowed further as her mind replayed every infraction Lilith committed. With the hate in her heart, it was hard to believe she once counted Lilith as one of her dearest friends. They had lived on Olympus together. In the past, the people assumed them to be the gods and goddesses. Temples rose and they became the subjects of myths. None of the vampires wanted the worship or that is what she understood then, but safety reigned. As long as the Greeks suspected them to be gods, they could live on Mount Olympus unharmed.

Sadly, the vampires there were the only family she knew. She did not remember her life before them. She had only remembered that they had offered her for a sacrifice. Instead of killing her, Ares had changed her and she had become reborn as Aphrodite. Her life before did not matter. Lilith had been known as Athena then and had been her constant companion.

She hadn't seen any ill will in Athena or maybe she didn't want to. She believed her to be a friend…a sister. When Aphrodite gave birth to Ares' son, Eros, it seemed Athena loved him…loved her, but she soon found she was very wrong. Athena had other reasons to love Eros. She wanted Ares and what better way to win him, than through his son.

One day her true intentions came to light when she tried to kiss Ares, causing Aphrodite to lose her temper. During the fight, it became known that Athena was angry that she had not been named the goddess of love and beauty. So, Aphrodite possessed everything Athena wanted…the title, Ares and the love of a son. She vowed to seek revenge upon Aphrodite and when she did Cronus banned her from Olympus. Another Athena came to take her place soon afterward.

A year passed and Aphrodite nearly forgot the pain Athena caused until she woke up one night to her scent. By the time she opened her eyes, it was too late. Athena had already exacted her revenge. Eros was gone.

Aphrodite and Ares searched for him, but years later they believed him to be dead because vampires did not birth vampires. They birthed mortals and his mortal years had passed.

Still, they continued to search, hoping to find Athena to mete out their revenge. Ares finally found her living under the name of Lilith. She lied to her followers claiming that she was the first vampire. That was laughable. Ares was centuries older than she was and Aphrodite a decade. Still, she'd gained followers. Most of them were too afraid of her to do anything but what she demanded. Her ruthlessness had become legendary.

That's how Ares found Athena. Her followers had told so many myths that he decided to see Lilith just in case she was a threat to the rest of the families. He found her in New York where she lived with a little girl. Ares was surprised when he had first laid eyes on her. She wasn't Lilith. She was Athena.

He would have attacked her then but he refused to put the little girl in danger. Eventually, Lilith did leave the little girl with her followers and Ares pursued her to Winchester, Tennessee. That's when he saw someone who he did not expect to see. When

50.
he told Aphrodite, she did not believed him. Ares had found their son who no longer went by the name Eros. Instead, he had adopted the monicker of Bernard. Ares had only known him because although he had been changed his scent was still the same. It was the sweet and heady mixture of both the scents of Aprhrodite and Ares.

A week past after Ares' revelation. Even though Aphrodite was skeptical, she knew that she had to see for herself...even if it would only end in heartbreak.

When she arrived in Winchester, she did find heartbreak in the years lost with her son. Ares had been right. He had found their child. Her heartbreak continued when she felt every stress that plagued him. She vowed to help him. So, as she watched him near the river, she couldn't help but to call out to him. She had to protect her son. She could not let Athena hurt him any longer. She had to call her out as the liar she was.

Aphrodite's nostrils flared as her blood burned through her veins. Soon, she would tell Bernard that she was his mother and she would rip Athena's heart from her chest. However, first she must find out what Athena was doing to her son. She looked up at the window that led to Athena's room and narrowed her eyes.

"Soon, you will die, Athena," Aphrodite whispered, "But first, I will torture you just like you have me."

She narrowed her eyes once more before turning and disappearing into the forest.

****

Marissa didn't expect her day to become so horrendous. All she wanted to do was to go for a run, the same as she did every morning. But as she came to the fork in the path, she realized that this morning was drastically different than any other. She understood that as soon as she found that she wasn't alone in the forest. She was approaching the fork in the path when she found a woman who was turned from her. Her head was bowed toward the large oak which marked the fork. Her shoulders were shaking and Marissa could hear heart-wrenching sobs echoing through the air.

Marissa slowed her pace before stopping a few feet from the woman and frowned in shock and concern as she took in the woman's appearance. She was dressed in blue jeans and a purple t-shirt that hugged her curves. Her head was bowed into her hands displaying a beautiful head of red, brown and gold hair. Marissa took a few steps toward her and raised her hands to show that she meant no harm as she neared the woman.

The woman's sobs sounded so distressed that Marissa's heart tightened in apprehension. She took another step toward her but the woman tensed before glancing at her. Marissa opened her mouth to speak but the woman turned and ran off of the path. Marissa's eyes widened in panic as she worried that she would become hurt or lost. She screamed for her not to go…that it was dangerous. Still, the woman ran and Marissa did not think to take her own advice. Instead, she followed her.

She did not see the woman for the first few moments and almost turned back. Then, through the trees she saw a flash of the woman's purple shirt and followed her. She chased after her until Marissa found herself in an unfamiliar part of the forest. The woman was nowhere in sight. Worse, against every bit of advice she had ever been given about being lost, she began to wander. She falsely assumed she could find her way back to the path. She had too much faith in her familiarity with the woods.

Hours passed but Marissa still walked further and futher into the forest, hoping to find something familiar but there was nothing. Nightfall came when true panic set into her soul. Every noise made Marissa jump, terrified. She ran mindlessly through the trees, hoping to find something familiar. She prayed that she would find her way out but every turn looked the same and following the stream proved hopeless because of the many forks and turns. Finally, she stopped and sat on a large boulder near the stream and sobbed.

Marissa trembled as the forest darkened even more. Terror made her heart beat hard within her chest. Dirt streaked her face and hands. Holes marred her clothes from falling or being snagged on branches. She looked down at her shirt noticing a tear down the front.

I am so stupid, she thought as images of her mother crying over her lifeless corpse came to mind. With a shiver, she pushed those thoughts away, hoping to never allow her mind to return to them again.

Laughter reached her and another wave of terror entered her soul. She looked around, tensing with the need to run again but it was too late. The woman who had been sobbing by the tree stood in front of her, smiling. Marissa's eyes widened as a frissure of fear worked up her spine telling her that the woman was dangerous and she needed to run.

"I suppose that our game has come to its end," she said, still smiling at Marissa and that's when Marissa saw them. Sharp canines longer than a mortal's pressed over her bottom lip. Marissa's eyes widened as she thought of what the woman was.

"Vampire," she whispered, terrified beyond any fear she had ever experienced.

It seemed as if every nightmare she had dreamed during the month after her near drowning was coming back to haunt her. She swallowed, knowing the difference. This was no dream. She was awake and monsters were real.

"Oh...The game is definitely over," the vampiress said, clapping her hands together happily. It was then that Marissa made the mistake of looking in the vampiress' eyes. Her mouth dropped open as she watched them change from brown to blue, swirling both colors before becoming solid. A tremble worked through Marissa. If there had been any doubt that the woman was a monster, it faded in an instant.

Finally, survival kicked into her mind and she stumbled backwards over the boulder, struggling to her feet before turning and running. Tears burned her eyes as she ran and then, stumbled, twisting her ankle. Still, she ran on the pained foot, determined to get away.

She had gotten through the first line of trees and had assumed for an instant that she was escaping when a dull pain slammed into the side of her head. She fell facedown onto the ground. The vampiress turned her over, laughing as she did.

"You shouldn't have run," she said, smiling, "Now, it will be much more painful for you."

The vampiress' teeth flashed as she pushed against Marissa's temple, pushing her head to the side and exposing her neck. She tried to fight but the vampiress was too strong. Finally, she just closed her eyes, accepting her fate. She would die and no one would find her.

Tears burned Marissa's eyes as the vampiress' breath touched her neck. She squeezed her eyes shut tighter, awaiting the pain. The points of the vampiress' canines pushed into the flesh of her neck nearly piercing the skin but then, the vampiress was...gone.

Marissa opened her eyes, blinking her vision clear after holding them closed so tightly. That's when she saw that the vampiress had vanished but she wasn't alone. For a moment, she only stared at the people around her. A doll-like woman and a large woman with spiraling hair came toward her. They put their hands out showing their intent not to harm. Two men stepped toward her, one she recognized and one she didn't…The one she didn't recognize stood tall but elegant and handsome though not nearly as handsome as the one who stood beside him.

Marissa said *his* name as a shiver worked through her, "Nicolas."

"Are you hurt?" He asked, frowning down at her, worried. Still, she didn't answer because she was wondering if she had died or maybe she had become ill or worse gone insane.

He leaned down and grasped her shoulders pulling her up until she stood in front of him. Her eyes rose until she looked into his face. He repeated his question, "Marissa, are you hurt?"

She swayed as dizziness hit her hard and she began to sink into darkness. She fought to stay awake, afraid that he would return to being just a dream.

She reached out and brushed her fingers over his cheek and somewhere within the darkness clouding around her, the realization came, "You're real," she whispered before darkness took her into its grip.

Chapter Five
Monsters and Angels

Marissa had no idea how long she had slept but it seemed like an eternity had passed. Slowly, she began to wake little by little. Even though she had yet to open her eyes, she realized almost immediately that she wasn't alone. She could feel others near as she struggled to pull her eyelids upward. When she found that she couldn't, she didn't fight it. Instead, she listened intently to the sounds around her, trying to hear who was with her and who was not.

Her stomach flipped at the thought and she tried to ignore

56.

the reason for her distress but it was there in glaring reality, whether she wanted to see it or not. She was afraid if she did awaken, she would find that the one good thing about her experience in the forest would be gone.

I couldn't have imagined him, she thought, desperately. Still, she realized that the thought wasn't true. She very well could have imagined him. She had been imagining him for months. At least, she thought she had been until she saw him in the forest. Her head began to pound. She knew it was too confusing to make sense of on her own. Worse, she realized that she would eventually have to face it. Still, she was going to wait awhile.

So, instead of opening her eyes, she listened to the sounds around her, hoping to recognize Nicolas' voice and trying to hold on to what was left of her sanity.

She didn't know how much time had passed but finally voices did come to her. She had to struggle to hear them at first because they sounded hollow as if they were coming to her from down a long tunnel and she was walking closer and closer to the end. She recognized her fourteen year old sister Karena's voice first. Worry laced her words as she spoke to her.

"Marissa, please wake up," Karena whispered to her. She felt her take her hand, "I know you can hear me."

Karena's voice made her forget her fear and Marissa tried to open her eyes but she slipped back into the darkness. Only her mother's voice roused her once more. Her voice was strained and Marissa knew that she had been crying.

"Marissa, why won't you wake up?" She asked with a tremor in her voice, "The doctor has seen you and can't find anything wrong."

Then, Marissa slipped into that darkness again. She no

longer wanted to fight it. She wanted to wake up. She couldn't put her family through this grief. If Nicolas wasn't real, she would face it. She struggled to force her eyes to open, finally pushing through the heaviness that pushed them closed and opening them wide. She blinked against the bright light. When her site cleared, she was surprised to find that she wasn't in the company of her family. Instead, she found herself in the presence of a woman who was large but beautiful with long, blonde hair which twisted and twirled down her back. She looked at Marissa with a raised quizzical brow.

"Who are you?" Marissa asked with a frown as familiarity crossed her conscience but she found no memory of the woman for that moment. She glanced around nervously searching for familiarity and noticed with relief that she stood on the porch of her home. The large wooden beams supporting the balcony rose above her, casting them both in its shadow. Slowly, she returned her gaze to the woman. Marissa frowned, confused. She was aware that she never saw the woman in her home but she stood there both familiar and unfamiliar. She knew without a doubt that she had met her somewhere.

She bit her lip as an understanding, vague but slowly coming to the surface of her mind, stretched across her sense of knowing until it bloomed into a rational idea. In a moment, Marissa realized she was dreaming.

The woman smiled with a knowledge that shouldn't be in the eyes of someone so young. After all, she was only a few years older than Marissa, "It doesn't matter who I am," she said finally answering Marissa's question in a voice with a slight French accent twisting within her words. She looked directly into Marissa's eyes and finally she realized with absolute certainty that she had seen this woman before. She even realized where. She had been one of the women with Nicolas in the forest. The woman continued, "You will meet me soon enough but your memory will not hold *this* meeting."

"I doubt that I'll forget," Marissa said, confused, "I usually don't forget much. Honestly, I don't understand why you want me to forget. I have a feeling that this is a dream."

The woman smiled as if amused, "Well, rest assured that you will forget me, dream or not."

Marissa didn't argue with her any further. She didn't see the point. The woman seemed to believe what she said and Marissa sensed she would argue with her if she disagreed. Instead, she asked, "What do you want from me?"

"Just what I said…I want you to forget," she said, bluntly. The smile that the woman had faded but kindness remained, "I want you to remember nothing of the woman in the forest who attacked you."

Marissa shivered and looked at the woman with wide eyes, "She's not a woman," she said, meeting the woman's eyes, "She's a vampire."

It shocked her that she admitted it so freely but she felt safe within the dream because if the woman judged her there, the judgement would not stretch into reality. She shrugged and continued, "Which is why I would never tell anyone anything. They would assume I lost my mind. Actually, I wonder that myself sometimes. After all, I've dreamed of Nicolas for months and I wonder if he is real or just a bit more of my imagination and now I'm speaking to another person who may or may not be a dream. I'm never quite sure. Maybe I *am* insane."

The woman pressed her lips together as her eyes flashed. Amusement was clear in her voice, "You aren't insane. I hope that means something.."

"I doubt that there is anything that you can do to prove my sanity right now...especially since you may or may not be a dream yourself," Marissa said and then, raised her eyebrows.

"I guess I see your point," the woman said crossing her arms over her ample chest.

Marissa gazed into her face and frowned, "I feel even more insane because even though I know that you may not be real, I need to ask you why *you* would want me to forget?"

The woman groaned, loosing all hint of amusement. Instead, frustration blanketed her face, "I will tell you but only because it's easier if you do not resist my suggestions," she said and hesitated before beginning again. Marissa could see that she was nervous, "The vampiress who attacked you will cause danger for myself but also for Nicolas and his family, if she is known."

"I definitely would not want that to happen," Marissa whispered as her stomach turned at the possibility but then, something else rooted in her mind and her stomach began to spin more.

"Why would it put you in danger?" Marissa asked but the woman seemed hesitant to tell her so she used the woman's own words to convince her, "It isn't like I'll remember when I wake up," she reminded the woman, "You said so yourself."

The woman bit her bottom lip nervously and sighed resigning. She opened her mouth a couple of times, closing it and then, deciding what to say, sighed again and then, spoke. Marissa had expected a great revealing. Instead, the woman asked her a question.

"Do you believe that in every creature there is both good and evil?" the woman asked, studying Marissa intently. Marissa's anticipation turned to confusion and disappointment. The revealing had not happened and she understood nothing of the woman's reasons from the question. Instead, she was left even more confused than she was before.

Marissa frowned at the woman and nodded her head, "Yes," she said, simply deciding to answer.

"Well, the vampire you met is evil. She's actually the purest evil. We fight against her," the woman said, hesitantly, "However…we are the same creature as she is. We are vampires."

Marissa's heart trembled and for a moment it was hard to breathe. What the woman said was a revelation, but not the one that she had wanted. Marissa looked at her with wide eyes, looking for fangs....looking for danger.

"Are you frightened?" The woman asked. She didn't seem a bit concerned and for a reason that Marissa couldn't name, the lady's demeanor calmed her to the point where she was able to speak.

"Are you going to hurt me?" Marissa asked as a tremble worked through her.

"No, we saved you," she said, laughing as if Marissa were being absurd, "We wouldn't do that if we were planning to harm you."

"Then, I'll *try* not to be frightened," Marissa said, swallowing down her fear.

"It doesn't matter," the woman said with a kind smile and a wave of a small hand, "Go back into the darkness and sleep peacefully. When you awaken, you'll not remember. Therefore, you will have nothing to be frightened of."

Marissa tried to fight the drugging heaviness that fell upon her but failed. The woman was making her fall into a deep sleep. However, she knew one thing that the woman would be unable to make her do and that was to make her forget. Oh, no. She would never forget but she also would never tell. She swallowed hard as she wondered if her sanity had taken another step into the darkness. If it had, when would she awaken into reality? If she wasn't insane, would she be able to love a vampire? She knew the answer only a second later. Yes. Yes, she would.

****

Bernard stared angrily at Lilith. The urge to strike out burned hot in his veins. He fought to keep his thoughts from Marissa and would only allow himself to consider the immense danger that he and Giselle were in. He trembled pushing Marissa's image to the back of his mind where Lilith wouldn't see her or realize his feelings because if she did, she would see his worry for her. He couldn't risk that, even though the vampiress had offered him help the morning before. If Lilith found out, she would order Marissa's death and then, it would be too late for her and his family. Lilith would destroy them all. Instead, he focused on her carelessness.

"You have put us all in danger!" He screamed, angrily. His hands were clenched into fists at his side as his nostrils flared, "All of it was for nothing more than your greed!"

Instead of seeming angry at his outburst, she was amused. A crooked grin rose on her face as she cocked a brow at him. For a moment, he had the insane need to slap her. He dug his nails into his palm so deeply that it drew blood. The scent surrounded them and she smiled evilly as she ran her tongue over her teeth. Her eyes met his and she cocked her head to the side as a chuckle bubbled up from her chest.

"And you're worried about mere mortals?" She asked, laughing. Her eyes flashed, mocking him for his human emotions. She was implying weakness in that. He narrowed his eyes as he stepped closer to her, trying to intimidate but failing.

62.
Lilith could not be intimidated.

"I don't see how you can't be," he growled, dangerously. She rose her chin unafraid of him as he continued to yell at her, "They'll come after us."

She had finally stopped laughing but had raised her brows studying him for a moment before she shrugged as if she did not have a care in the world, "I don't know why you are carrying on so badly," she said rolling her eyes. Her voice rang with boredom. Then, she smiled almost kindly but Bernard knew better than to fall for that smile even if her words dripped with sweetness, "Especially when I was trying to help my dear son. As always, you don't appreciate my kindness and that hurts me deeply."

He shook his head unfooled by her. After all, he had known her his whole life. She was anything but sweet or kind, "You've made everything worse," he said with anger boiling hot and deadly within him, "Now the Prestons will come for us. Their family will hunt us down and kill every single one of us. They'll call the families," he said through clenched teeth. Her face twisted in a pout of feined hurt. He shook his head as he called her out for her lies, "You didn't do this to help me. You did it to hurt me."

"I *was* trying to help you," she said as anger flooded her face, "I saw an opportunity to drain Marissa and I took it. It seemed that you were reluctant to do so and I assumed that it was because of those dreadful human emotions that you hold onto," she said and sighed, shaking her head making her hair shake slightly, "And as for the Prestons, I have decided to dispose of them. A war is long overdue. So, you can quit worrying about retribution."

His eyes widened in horror. He didn't want the Preston's

to die. Already, he had done such horrible things to them, "I won't condone it, much less fight in it," he said, turning from her, "It will kill us all. I refuse to do it."

She put her hand on his shoulder, turning him to face her. Her face was red in anger, "You *will* do as I say," she said and then, smiled, "Or have you forgotten *who* is at stake."

A tremble worked through him as the image of a little girl more important to him than anything else rose in his mind. He narrowed his eyes at her as thoughts of murder freely swept through his head.

Lilith's smile widened, "I just wanted to remind you," she said and turned walking to the door before turning to him once again, "Don't make me do something that *you'll* regret."

Then, she was gone, leaving him with his anger. He threw a vase at the door, expending only a little of his temper. He stood in the middle of the room as his breaths rushed in and out of his lungs. He stared at the door at a loss of what he could do. He only knew that he wanted Lilith dead but he didn't know how to attain that wish. He closed his eyes as desperation swept through him. A moment later, a sense of calm came along with the only hope he had.

"Bernard," the voice of a woman whispered inside his head. He recognized it from the morning before, "Don't be angry. Don't lose hope. Come meet us in the forest with your wife. We will stop her from harming anymore innocents. We will stop her from harming you."

Without another thought, he went in search of Giselle.

****

Ares stood with his arm around Aprhrodite's shoulders. She trembled slightly as they waited for their son to arrive with his wife in the forest. Ares himself could feel the sting of tears touch his light green eyes. He didn't know whether they were tears of relief or fear because he didn't know how Bernard would accept them. Aphrodite stiffened as Bernard's scent reached them.

"They're coming," she said in a voice which trembled in anticipation. She looked up at him with large blue eyes, "His bond is stronger than any other I've felt."

He understood what she meant. Ares was aware of his son too. He had never been so attuned to anyone, not even Aprhodite, who he loved more than his own existence.

He looked toward the trees where he felt them most anticipating the exact moment they would arrive. He closed his eyes for a moment and then, opened them the moment Bernard and his wife came into view. Ares eyes swept over Bernard, searching for likenesses between himself and his son. They shared the same golden blonde hair. He had his mother's blue eyes but Ares square face and long straight nose. His lips were full like Aprhodite's but he possessed Aries tall, muscular frame. Aries smiled as his heart clenched in love and pride because Bernard was a perfect mixture of Aphrodite and himself. He was the tribute to their love.

Aries forced his eyes away from Bernard to the woman beside him. She was a striking strawberry blonde with beautiful blue-green eyes. A pretty light green dressed hugged her slender frame. Her hair was perfectly combed and trimmed. She was astonishing.

He returned his gaze to Bernard. He noticed as they got closer, a look of recognition crossed his son's face. Ares eyes widened as he experienced hope bloom in his chest. Perhaps, he would believe them because of the recognition. Perhaps, there was something left of him and Aphrodite in Bernard's memory.

Aries hoped so.

"Bernard," Ares said as his son stood in front of him. He smiled widely at his son and then, turned to his wife, "I am glad you've come. My name is Ares and this is my wife, Aprhodite." He motioned toward her as he said her name.

Aphrodite had begun to twist the end her long wheat blonde hair around her finger, nervously, as she looked up at them. Another wave of recognition crossed Bernard's face but he shook himself.

"Obviously, you know who I am," Bernard said and then, turned to the woman beside him. He reached for his wife's hand and grasped it protectively in his, "This is my wife, Giselle."

"Your names are like the Greek gods," Giselle said with wide eyes. Her wariness seemed to fade as her gaze swept over them. Unfortunately, Bernard was still suspicious.

Ares smiled patiently. It seemed odd to have such a casual conversation at such an extremely stressful time, "We were thought to be them in Greece," he explained, "We lived on Mount Olympus and the people noticed we were different. It was their way of explaining our strangeness. We couldn't correct them for obvious reasons."

Bernard frowned as another wave of recognition passed through him and into Ares. He was sure that Aphrodite sensed it too because she visibly stiffened. He tightened his arm around her slender shoulders hoping to calm her.

"You recognize us on some level, don't you?" Aphrodite asked Bernard. Aries' eyes widened in panic but he said nothing. Instead, his gaze returned to his son as worry and anticipation raced through him.

Bernard didn't answer. Instead, he studied her slowly. He took in her long blonde hair and bright blue eyes, the same shade

66.

as his own. His gaze lowered to her buttoned nose and full lips. Then, he looked at Ares following the same path down his face.

"I do recognize you, though I can't place from when or where," Bernard said, frowning, "I only know that I've seen you before."

"I've known you since your birth," Ares said, softly, hoping to dispell the suspicion in his eyes.

"I've known you a little longer than that," Aphrodite said, placing her hand on her stomach. Ares tightened his arm around her shoulders again, but this time in warning to explain slowly. It would be enough of a shock to Bernard without blurting it out.

"And because of this, you want to help me," Bernard said, shaking his head, "I apologize but I don't understand why you would want to help me?" he asked as he shifted nervously. Guilt blanketed his face, "Especially, since I know that I don't deserve it...after everything I've done."

Aries' placed his hand over his heart. He sympathized with his son. Bernard hadn't wanted to do the evil he had done. He had been forced by Lilith.

"Maybe I can explain," Ares said ignoring the thickness in his voice. Instead, he met Bernard's eyes, holding his gaze, "What do you know of Lilith?"

Bernard seemed taken aback by the question, but still, he answered, "That she's the first vampire," he said, softly, "That she was the first wife of Adam and didn't want to be subservient to him. She was turned into a vampire as punishment."

Ares had to suppress a laugh. The vampiress he had known as Athena had lied well. Still, it surprised him at how easily she was believed, "What if I told you that I know that to be untrue?" He asked, careful to keep eye contact with Bernard, "Would you believe me?"

"It would depend," Bernard said, looking at him with wide eyes. Confusion and suspicion shined within them but there was also hope, "How would you know that?"

"I was changed before her. I knew her when she was just a fledgling," Ares answered with a strained smile, "She was changed by Zeus and given the name Athena. She is only about a decade younger than Aphrodite. I am much older than both of them."

Bernard's mouth opened in astonishment. He seemed to search for something to say. His breaths were moving in and out of his body in harsh gasps. Tears rested in his eyes as he opened his mouth obviously searching for words to describe how he felt. Still, he was at a loss. Instead, it was Giselle who spoke.

"She lied?" Giselle asked, angrily and when Ares nodded his head she gave a snort of disapproval, "Why is that not surprising? She always lies."

"But why would a lie about who she is cause you to want to help me?" Bernard asked, recovering from his shock fairly quickly. Obviously, Lilith had lied so many times that Bernard wasn't surprised by her untruths any longer.

"It's not because of the lies that we want to help you," Ares said, looking into his son's eyes, "It's because of something of far greater importance. You'll understand when you are ready to listen. I must ask...is that time now?" Bernard tilted his head, studying Ares before he nodded for him to continue. Ares took a deep breath and then, spoke as carefully as he could, "We knew Lilith as Athena. She lived with us on Olympus. She was our friend...or we thought she was until a little time after Aphrodite and I had a son. When he was three years old, Lilith took him from us because she was angry that Aphrodite had the title of goddess of love and beauty. Also, she tried to win me but I love

Aphrodite," Ares said as a tremble shook him, "We searched for our son but we believed he had died because his mortal years had passed, but we found that not to be true. Lilith changed him. He still walks the earth."

It only took a moment for Bernard to understand, "Am I your son?" He asked. It surprised Ares to see hope light in his eyes. Still, he hesitated before answering him.

"Please, tell me," Bernard pleaded, "Am I your child?"

"You are," Ares said, watching as Bernard cupped his hands over his face in relief and surprise. His shoulders shook as he sighed. When he raised his head, tears shined in his eyes. He gazed at Aphrodite.

"I think I remember you," he whispered, "You're familiar...You're my mother?"

Aprhodite nodded, "You are my son," she said, stepping forward and caressing Bernard's cheek with one shaking hand. Tears flowed freely down her cheeks as she whispered, "Not hers."

Bernard took a shaky breath as his eyes narrowed, "That's why she's tortured me," he said as his mind finally took in everything. He took a step back and looked at Giselle with a realization that both grieved and angered him. Fury fumed on both of their faces. "She's tortured me and made me do things that every ounce of my soul hates. When she could no longer force me to do those things, she found a way to punish me if I didn't."

"What has she done, Bernard?" Ares asked, experiencing his own anger. Bernard glanced at him suddenly panicked.

"She's taken our daughter, Bridget," he said, as tears welled in his eyes, "We have no idea where she is. She's holding her until I give in. She's forcing me to do something that I don't want to do."

Bernard sank down to sit in the grass as tears flowed in jagged lines down his cheeks. Giselle leaned down next to him to embrace him protectively against her breast.

"What is she trying to make you do?" Aphrodite asked as her eyes widened in worry.

It was Giselle who raised her gaze to Aphrodite. Her face reddened as she answered through clenched teeth, "There is a girl, who looks exactly like me. Her name is Marissa Dalene. Her parents are wealthy," Giselle said as her own eyes threatened to overflow but she blinked the tears back, "She wants Bernard to become her boyfriend so Lilith can get close enough to drain her and her family. I would take her place as the only surviving heir. Lilith would then take control of the money. We don't want that to happen. However, if we don't do as she has ordered, she'll change Bridget," Giselle said and began to sob, "She's only seven years old."

Ares' eyes narrowed as a memory came to him. In New York, Lilith had been with a blonde headed little girl. She had left her there in the care of her followers. He searched Bernard's mind for an image of the little girl and immediately realized that the little girl in New York and Bridget were one and the same.

"I saw her," Ares said, smiling when everyone looked at him with wide eyes, "She's in New York. That's where Lilith was before she came here. I can get her."

Giselle stood and went to him. She gazed up at him with wide eyes, "To lie to us would be cruel."

"I'm not lying," he said, glancing at his wife, his son and then, his daughter-in-law, "But we have to be careful. Lilith can not know. You must act as you always have because if she believes that you've turned on her, then she'll kill Marissa and she wouldn't hesitate to kill or change Bridget either. I will need some help but I'll get it within a week, maybe two. I will try to get her before Lilith forces you to do anything to Marissa. I promise."

"What if you don't get to her in time?" Giselle asked, narrowing her eyes. Aries felt his stomach turn. He was determined that this scenario would not happen. Still, he knew they needed a plan just in case. He stared into Bernard's eyes.

"If we don't get back soon enough, you'll have to change her and hide her," Ares said, "Lilith must believe she died."

"We don't want to do that," Giselle said, horrified.

Aries swallowed over the guilt of the words but he realized this was the only choice if he could not retrieve Bridget in time, "Lilith is too observant. She'll notice that you don't have the smell of Marissa's blood on you. If she orders her death and I'm not back with Bridget, you will have to drain her to the point of death for Lilith to believe you. The only option after that is to change her. I understand it's a difficult choice but at least this way she'll exist," Ares said, softly and then added reassuringly, "I will try to do this quickly. So, hopefully it won't come to that."

Bernard nodded, "At least now we have a chance. We can get Bridget back and Marissa can be okay," he whispered, "We have hope. We didn't have that before."

Bernard gave a small smile to his father and for the first time since Ares had laid eyes upon him in his adulthood, he saw relief shining within the blue depths of his eyes. Ares placed his hand on his chest as an ache settled there. He realized that it wouldn't fade until he retrieved Bridget for Bernard. He could only hope that he wouldn't disappoint him. In that moment, he promised himself that his son would soon experience nothing but happiness and hope in his future. In the darkest part of his heart, he made another promise. Lilith would pay for every single offense against him and his family.

Chapter Six
Decisions and Awakenings

Thalia narrowed her eyes as she looked out of the window of her living room toward the Dalene's house across the street. She couldn't deny that she was afraid but more than that she was worried for Marissa. She kept seeing her image over and over again at different ages in her life...Only each image ended with her corpse drained of blood and lying in a casket. It was like a morbid movie replaying in her head but there was no stop button. It only played over and over again.

Still there seemed to be one living image of Marissa that

she kept coming back to. It was of the first time Thalia held her. She had been named her godmother. In that moment, she had promised to always protect her and when Karena came and she was given the same honor, she made the same promise to her too. It was a promise she made often to her own children. She didn't take it lightly.

Concern creased her brow as she continued to watch the house. Fear trembled through her at the idea of Marissa alone in the forest. Anything could have happened. Still, she knew there was only one thing she was truly worried about. Marissa was smart. She would have made it out of the forest under normal circumstances but...

He could've killed her no one would have known, her mind whispered, offering her worst fear as tears burned her eyes. She sighed heavily as she tried to push the thought away.

"Momma, what's wrong?" Her son, Thomas asked interrupting her thoughts. He had been speaking to her as she gazed at the Dalene's house but she didn't remember one thing that he said.

She tensed. Her family knew what Bernard was. Thomas was the only one who didn't believe her. Still, she wouldn't lie to him.

"I'm thinking about Marissa," she said, turning to him. She gazed at him, hoping that for once he would understand but she realized that he probably wouldn't.

Her gaze swept over him. He was a slender but muscled boy of fifteen. He possessed dark brown hair and his eyes shined so dark that they were nearly black. His skin was the color of freshly ground coffee. He reminded her so much of her husband, William when he was young. As he looked at her with a furrowed brow, he reminded her of William more than ever.

"The doctor says she's fine," he said, softly and even though he continued to speak, she realized he was dismissing her worries, "He said that she's in shock and needs time to wake up but she *will* wake up."

"*He* could have killed her," Thalia whispered, hoping to get through to him.

Thomas' face hardened and he turned away from her. She knew that he still didn't believe her. He probably never would.

"Mother, this has got to stop," he said, sternly as he shook his head, "There are no such things as vampires. It's crazy to think that there is."

She frowned at him, heartbroken and turned from him trying to suppress the tears that had risen to her eyes again.

He called for her and when she didn't turn to face him, he sighed. Then, the door opened and she assumed he left but a moment later, Eliza's voice came to her.

"What did you do to her?" Eliza demanded in a tone that she only used when she was being protective.

She turned at the harshness of Eliza's words. She was thirteen and as much as Thomas looked like William, Eliza looked like Thalia but younger and thinner. She had the same caramel colored skin and tanned eyes. She had her large bosom and black hair with copper colored strands running through it.

"I didn't do anything to her," Thomas said defensively, "She began talking about vampires and I told her to stop…They aren't real."

"Why must she stop?" Eliza asked, stubbornly, "Because *you* don't take her at her word?"

"And you do?" Thomas scoffed. He gave her a look that implied that she was entertaining childish notions. Eliza must have noticed because she narrowed her eyes, stepping in front of him defensively.

"Don't treat me like a child, just because you're two years older than me, Thomas Sorenson," She said, poking him in the chest, "Let me ask you this, when has our mother lied to us? When has she ever acted as if she lost her senses?"

Thomas frowned and Eliza smiled, "That's right, Thomas," She said, smugly, "You can't tell me when she's lied to us because she never has. Perhaps, you should quit acting as if you know everything and go find our father instead of making our mother feel badly."

Thomas stumbled for words. When he found nothing to say, he left the room as Eliza had told him to do. Thalia smiled weakly at her stubborn daughter.

"You shouldn't have been so rough," Thalia sighed, "It *is* hard to believe."

"It shouldn't be," Eliza replied, "Like I said to Thomas, you've never lied to us."

Thalia swallowed hard, "No, and I shouldn't be lying to Marissa either."

Eliza frowned, "What do you mean?"

"As soon as Marissa is home, I'm telling her about Bernard Talbot," She said, waiting for her daughter to protest.

Instead, Eliza put her arms around Thalia's shoulders, "Well, if she doesn't believe you, then tell her to come talk to me."

Thalia put her arms around her child, hugging her close, relieved that one of her children didn't view as insane. She only hoped that Marissa would have faith in her sanity too.

****

Abigail could sense herself falling as the vision took hold. Her eyes rolled back so far that pain throbbed throughout her head. She gasped. The vision had taken her so quickly that she was thankful she had returned to the Preston's home. Otherwise, she would have had the vision in front of every member of the Dalene family and that would have been not only embarrassing but a tragedy.

The vision hit her harder than ever and she found herself very frightened as she fell further and further into darkness. She trembled as she prepared herself. She tried to remain calm by remembering that even if this one was frightening, the visions weren't always exact. Sometimes, they were steeped in symbols that would only reveal themselves right before an event would happen. Still, no comfort came because she didn't think this would be one of those dreams.

As she fell into this vision, she found it different than the others. Darkness enveloped her so quickly that she had the sensation of floating. When she found her feet on solid ground, it was surreal. The darkness surrounding her like a cloak did not help her to dispel the feeling. Worse, the inability to see had *never* happened in a vision before.

She looked around, blinking in the darkness. A frown marked her brow as she tensed, awaiting danger. She realized that it was probably a defense mechanism that she had long forgotten. After all, she had not had trouble seeing in the darkness since she was a mortal. Still, it shocked her how terrifying the complete darkness could be. She frowned at the intensity of the feeling realizing that the fear must have faded in all of her years of mortality and because of that, she was remembering the sensation with terrifying intensity. She took a deep breath, as she tried to push the fear away and narrowed her eyes as she strained to see in the darkness.

Panic almost set in, but she began to detect outlines of

shadows and she sensed other vampires near. She inhaled finding the comforting scents of her family close to her, but there were other scents that swirled around her getting closer and closer which did not belong to family.

She blinked again and a change happened which calmed her. The colors began to fill in and a brightness began to come, not unlike the sun rising. She glanced around the forest first and then, she began to recognize all the smaller families which made up her large family. She saw her French family, the one which she and Anrique were the leaders of. She saw the Greek and Irish parts of her family and she sensed even more. However, the part of her family which caught her attention were the Prestons. She realized only one missing from them…Nicolas. She glanced around searching for him sure that this vision had something to do with him. She scanned the crowd but stopped when she spotted a familiar face within the crowd. Her eyes widened as she thought she saw Marissa. Abigail tried to walk closer to be sure but the vision held her back. Instead, she could only view the girl from a distance.

Abigail's gaze swept over her landing on a bundle held protectively in her arms. She blinked in surprise as she realized that the girl was holding a baby. Her eyes moved back up to the girl's face and she inhaled sharply. Abigail was not mistaken. The girl *was* Marissa.

What shocked her was there was a vampiress that stood directly across from her that looked exactly like her. Abigail frowned as she noticed that the vampiress held the hand of a vampire who looked distinctly familiar but his face was turned away. Abigail walked closer and the familiarity grew.

Slowly, the vampire turned. Her eyes widened as she realized that it was Bernard. Instantly, she knew the identity of

78.

the vampiress...Giselle. She looked behind them and noticed Lilith's family marching up behind Bernard and his mate. Then, Marissa did something that made Abigail's stomach turn. Danger prickled down her neck and slid down her spine as Marissa lifted her hand and offered it to Giselle.

"Marissa, No!" She screamed but Marissa did not pull away. Instead, she grasped Giselle's hand tightly in hers. Abigail gasped as she gazed at them in panic. She could feel her blood rushing through her veins.

She braced herself for their attack but the attack never came. Instead, Marissa pulled both Bernard and Giselle behind her as if she were protecting them. Another gasp escaped Abigail as she watched the scene.

Abigail walked toward them getting closer and closer. She stood near enough that she could clearly see everything they were doing. Her eyes traveled downward and she jerked in shock to find a little girl with blonde hair and deep blue eyes clutching Giselle's hand. Instinctively, Abigail knew that the little girl belonged to her. Giselle was the little girl's mother.

Abigail's attention returned to Marissa when she took the baby in her arms and gently placed the bundle into Giselle's waiting hands. Abigail took another step. The breath left her body as she was able to really see Marissa for the first time. Her mouth opened in shock as she took in her face. She was different and Abigail knew why. Marissa was no longer mortal. She had been changed. Abigail's eyes widened as she continued to walk, stopping only fifteen feet from Marissa and Bernard. Just then, the war broke out. The families warred with each other brutally, but Bernard and Marissa weren't joining in the fight and Giselle had run from the brutality with the children tucked protectively against her.

Abigail scanned Bernard who was facing Marissa. He reached out and caressed her cheek and looked at her almost lovingly before pulling away. His hand moved toward his belt and pulled something from it. It flashed in the sun. Abigail narrowed her eyes, seeing what he held…a knife, ornate and golden. Slowly, he handed it to Marissa before giving her a pained look as he backed away, watching her closely. Marissa was looking down at the knife with determination in her eyes. Abigail blinked in awe but when she opened her eyes, Marissa and Bernard were no longer there.

Abigail began to search. It seemed like hours passed before she realized that something had changed. Before, a war had been waged and vampires fought violently. As she looked around she realized the fighting had stopped. Everything had become deadly silent and she noticed that all the vampires surrounded one area.

Abigail walked toward the crowd and made her way to the front trying to be cautious that no one attacked her. When she reached the center of the crowd, she found the reason for the sudden silence. Marissa stood in front of her grasping her stomach as blood poured from between her fingers. Still, she tried to release the bonds around Nicolas' hands. He too was hurt, though it seemed that he fared much better than Marissa. Abigail looked for the source of their wounds and found it fairly quickly.

Lilith lay on the ground with the ornate knife protruding from her chest. Her life's blood soaked into the ground below her and already she was turning to ash. Abigail looked back at Marissa. The deathblow had been delivered by Marissa. Slowly, Abigail walked toward her, grateful that she had saved many of her family. She sliced open her wrist as she walked toward Marissa to offer her healing blood to her, but the dream disintegrated, leaving her grasping her chest.

Abigail rose within the opulent bedroom that Elizabeth had given her and went to the window. She put her hand on it, projecting to Marissa.

Don't worry, Marissa. You will not die for your kindness, she promised. She narrowed her eyes, trying to remember every aspect of the vision so that not one hair on Marissa's head would be harmed. Abigail took a deep breath and then, turned toward the door to return to Marissa as her guard.

****

Marissa felt the heaviness lift from her. Light came to her, looking red behind her eyelids. Still, she left them closed as she forced her mind to recall each thing that had happened to her. Everything began to fall into place so quickly that her heart began to pound.

Could everything have really happened?

She opened her eyes and found herself in a hospital room. The smell of alcohol assaulted her and she wrinkled her nose. The room was sterile and white…too white. A dry erase board was across from her and she frowned as she read the words *Lisa will be your nurse today.* She turned her head and found tubes connected to her through an IV or to the machine that beeped with each beat of her heart.

She turned and found the woman from her dream with the spiraling blonde locks sitting in a chair beside her bed. It took everything in her power not to gasp in shock.

The woman is real, she thought but then, her heart sank, *If the woman is real, then, Nicolas is real and so are vampires. They were vampires.*

She blinked as she realized again that it did not matter. She loved him.

"I didn't mean to frighten you, Marissa," the woman said, regaining her attention, "I was watching over you while you slept. My name is Abigail Dubois. I was with the family who found you in the forest."

Marissa studied the woman. She had believed that she had made Marissa forget. Marissa glanced at the woman's teeth, seeing no fangs and then looked back up into her green eyes.

"Where's Nicolas?" Marissa asked and the woman frowned as worry touched her face.

"Nicolas?" She asked, stepping closer to her, studying her with an intensity that should have made Marissa uncomfortable.

"Yes, Nicolas," Marissa said, stubbornly raising her chin, "I want to see him."

Abigail stared at her for a moment as if trying to see into her soul. Marissa swallowed and again looked at her teeth. Abigail's frown deepened and her lips thinned.

"What do you remember from the forest?" Abigail asked. Marissa frowned. Why would Abigail worry that she hadn't forgotten when she had only asked for Nicolas? Marissa's eyes narrowed further as she realized that she had tried to make her forget the man she loved. *How dare she?*

"Why would I remember anything, when you've tried so hard to make me forget?" Marissa asked, angrily.

Abigail frowned, "I won't deny it. I don't see the point now," she said, coming closer to the bed. Abigail narrowed her eyes. When she spoke again her voice softened and held something like respect in its tone, "Ive never met a mortal like you. No mortal has ever been able to remember what I've told them to forget," she whispered almost to herself. Then, she looked at Marissa with a pleading look on her face, "I hope that you understand I've done these things to protect my family...and you."

"I would never do anything to harm any of you…especially Nicolas," Marissa replied calming. She could see the guilt mixing with the fear on Abigail's face, "And I wouldn't tell anything about the vampire in the forest. When it comes to myself, I believe that I have every right to make my choice in what degree of danger I put myself into."

A frown crossed Abigail's face, "What do you remember of my…visit with you?"

Marissa smiled, nervously, "I remember everything," she whispered, "I know what you are," Absolute horror crossed Abigail's face and she couldn't help but to quickly add, "But you shouldn't be afraid," Marissa looked up at her with a raised brow, feeling tired of the useless banter between them, "Now, can I see Nicolas?"

Abigail trembled for a moment as she looked toward the door. She seemed uncertain as to what to do. She looked back at Marissa straightening as she did.

"You're mother and father will want to speak with you first," Abigail said anxiously.

"Maybe everyone should come in," Marissa said, exasperated, "Then, when everyone hears my explanation, they'll see they have no reason to worry."

Abigail nodded her head and left the room. A moment later , the first of her family arrived. Her sister, Karena bounded into the room making the room seem to burst from her energy. Even at fourteen, she possessed an exotic beauty, with chestnut colored hair and pale skin. Her eyes were the same blue-gree as Marissa's with flecks of gold in them. Sometimes, they looked almost yellow. She had a short, straight nose and full lips that seemed to pout even when she wasn't upset. Even at fourteen, she had developed curves that Marissa envied but she loved her more than her own life and she couldn't imagine any form of jealousy changing that.

"Marissa, you scared us half to death," she said, "Why did you go so far into the forest?"

"I would like to know that myself," Thalia's voice, drifted to her from the doorway.

Marissa's swallowed hard as she looked at Thalia. Dark rings marked her eyes. It was obvious that she hadn't slept.

Behind her came her father, Josiah Dalene. He was a strong man who emitted just as strong a presence. His hair shared the same shade of strawberry blonde as Marissa's but his skin was tanned from working with his workers on crops. His eyes were a bright blue. He had a narrow, straight nose and lips that were a little thin when he smiled. His face was oval and seemed strong and chiseled especially around the cheeks and jaw. When Marissa looked up into his eyes she saw that worry glinted in them.

Thalia's husband, William walked in directly behind him. His dark, square face was lined in worry. His dark eyes swept over her and finally a small smile broke across his face. His teeth looked extremely white next to his dark skin. As he walked past her, he caressed her face for a moment.

"You scared us, Little one," he said and Marissa looked up at him apologetically before he went to stand next to her father.

Her mother, Helena arrived next. She was regal in appearance. Her chestnut colored hair was pulled back into a perfect bun. She stood perfectly straight but her face was lined in worry and her eyes looked red from lack of sleep or from crying.

Then, came Abigail and the doll-like woman who had also been within the forest protecting Marissa. Again, Marissa could not help but to look at the small woman's teeth in search of fangs but found none. The woman twisted her hands frantically in front of her. Marissa viewed the action as odd because it was something that any number of normal people might do when they were nervous. Obviously, Abigail had told her that Marissa remembered everything.

The tall gentleman with the emerald eyes entered next, looking just as nervous as the doll-like woman who he flanked protectively. At least he didn't twist his hands. He looked toward Marissa and tried to smile but it looked more like a grimace.

Then her eyes fell on the last person to enter…Nicolas. Her breath nearly caught in her throat as she stared at him, searching for one difference in his appearance from when she saw him in the dreams but there were none. He nearly reached out to her when he stood beside her bed, but stopped himself before anyone but her would notice. She looked up at him and smiled, nervously.

"I guess you are wondering who these people are," her mother said, looking at each of them with gratitude clear on her face. Marissa broke her gaze from Nicolas and looked into her mother's wary eyes.

"I think they are the one's who saved me," Marissa said, softly, "They look vaguely familiar."

"They are," her father said as she turned her gaze on him. He waved his hand toward the emerald eyed man, "This is Frazier Preston."

Frazier stepped forward and took Marissa's hand in his, gently, "I'm so glad that we found you," he said and then, gently took his hand from hers and waved it toward the doll-like woman, "This is my wife, Elizabeth. She has been waiting to meet you."

Elizabeth's hands stopped twisting but still, she shook.

Marissa tried to smile reassuringly at her, "It is very nice to meet you," Marissa said, "I hope that we can be friends."

"I would like that," Elizabeth said in a wonderfully musical voice.

Marissa turned her gaze to Abigail, "I have met Mrs. Dubois," Marissa said a bit too sweetly, "She was here when I woke."

Abigail gave her another pleading look, but Marissa turned her gaze to Nicolas.

Let her be frightened, Marissa thought, *Maybe she won't try to erase my memories again.*

Marissa looked up at Nicolas and then heard her father's introduction, "This is Nicolas Preston," her father said, "He's the man who nearly got shot when he carried you into our home."

"Daddy, you didn't harm him when he only wanted to help me?" Marissa scolded looking at him, alarmed.

"No, I didn't," he said and shrugged, "But only because he had a quick explanation."

Marissa looked back at Nicolas and shook her head, "I apologize, Mr. Preston," she said and then smiled, "My father can sometimes be a bit...overprotective."

"It is understandable," Nicolas said, softly, "I would be protective of you too."

Marissa blushed, looking down for a moment and hoped that no one within the room had noticed.

"Marissa," her mother said, softly, "I know that you've been through such a horrible ordeal but I must know how you got lost in the forest."

Marissa turned her gaze to her mother, glancing at Elizabeth first. She was again twisting her hands together. There was something about the small woman that made Marissa want to protect her. Slowly, she looked into her mother's eyes.

"It was completely stupid," Marissa said, looking at her mother, "I wanted to find a new path to run. The old one I was following ended and I decided to go off the path because I thought I knew my way. I got lost. I was so frightened. When the Prestons came, I passed out in relief.

Her mother looked at her with a frown. Marissa knew that she was searching for a lie within her story. She stubbornly held her mother's gaze. Finally, she sighed and Marissa looked down, "Do not ever do anything like that again," her mother scolded, "You could have been killed."

"I'm sorry, Mother," Marissa said, looking at Elizabeth, who had finally stopped her constant twisting. Marissa turned her gaze back to her mother, "I didn't mean to get lost and I realize how terribly childish it was. I promise that I won't ever do it again."

Her mother caressed her cheek and smiled weakly, "I'm just happy that you are safe," her mother leaned forward and kissed her cheek, "But perhaps now you should rest."

"I would like to thank my rescuers, first," Marissa said and then looked at Abigail and smiled, "I think that it would be impolite for me to… *forget* them."

Abigail winced but recovered so quickly that no one noticed. Marissa's mother leaned forward and kissed her forehead before leaving the room with the warning not to exert herself. Her father quickly returned to work with William on his heels and Karena left with Thalia to stay with her for the day.

When she was sure that her family was gone, Marissa sat up amongst her blankets and pillows. Nicolas stepped forward cautiously, "Marissa…"

Marissa raised her hand to stop him, "I don't understand

everything that has happened and at this point, I'm too tired to try," Marissa said, looking up at him, "But I'll have questions when I am feeling myself again."

"I'm sure that you do," Abigail whispered and Marissa narrowed her eyes at her.

"And because I have had to lie for you," Marissa continued, raising her brow, "You *will* answer them."

Each of the Preston's looked at her suspiciously and Marissa saw something else on their faces that made a shudder go down her spine. After all, what could terrify a vampire?

Chapter Seven
Innocence Lost

Giselle looked out of the window of the bedroom she shared with Bernard with tears standing in her eyes. She closed her eyes focusing on Bridget. A tremble worked through her as Bridget's tear-stricken face came before her.

"You'll come home to us soon," she whispered, brokenly, "I promise."

Bridget's image faded and Giselle had to stop the scream of anguish from issuing from her lips. If Lilith heard that, she would make her suffering even worse. She always did. It angered Giselle and sometimes, she thought that she was being punished for her actions because at one time, Giselle had been as cold and cruel as Lilith.

Since Bridget's birth, something had happened to her. When she looked down into her little angel's face for the first time, something broke in her and she cried. In her long life, she never remembered crying, but she did then.

It shamed her, but it was the first time that she had experienced love since she was a little girl. She hadn't loved Bernard, until then. She hadn't loved anyone. Since then Giselle loved and to Bridget, she gave her heart.

Still, she couldn't show it. She hated to be cruel, but she must. If Lilith saw any emotion from her or Bernard, she made them pay for it. She wouldn't put her daughter in jeopardy or Bernard. She couldn't because she truly loved them and because of that she couldn't show her true self to Nicolas when he visited because there was too much of a risk that she would be discovered. The only person she showed her true self to was Bernard.

A hand closed on her shoulder and she jumped, "Don't worry," Bernard said, softly, "It's only me."

She turned to him burying her head in his chest, feeling the panic rise, "I'm so frightened for her."

"I know," Bernard said, closing his arms around her tighter, "So am I."

"Promise me that everything will be alright," Giselle pleaded in sobs.

Bernard swallowed, "Everything *will* be alright," he whispered but even as he said it, worry coated his voice.

He closed his eyes, but a moment later she sensed danger

prickling through him and into her. His eyes flew open just as the door swung inward. Lilith walked in with a smirk on her face. Bernard quickly shielded his thoughts and Giselle's thoughts closed off also.

"Tears," Lilith said, raising her brow and then shook her head making her hair cascade in brown, red and blond waves, "Human emotions."

She shook her head again tsking and Giselle's temper rose.

"What do you want, Mother?" Bernard spat out.

" We have new vampires near us. Some that create a potential threat," She said, stepping forward and narrowing her eyes at both Giselle and Bernard.

Bernard frowned and looked at Giselle before he looked back at Lilith. Giselle's eyes widened, realizing for the first time that worry did cross Lilith's brow. For a moment, she nearly smiled. *Who was having human emotions now?*

"Who?" Bernard asked, swallowing. Giselle bit her bottom lip at his nervousness. A moment later, she understood why he was so worried.

"They're part of a Greek band that I knew long ago," she said and a strange smile spread across her lips, "Their names are Aphrodite and Ares."

Bernard's face paled. Keeping his mind blocked was painful, torturous, she knew. She had to do something quickly before Lilith realized how upset he had become.

"Like the Greek Gods?" Giselle asked, smoothly, keeping Lilith from looking too closely at Bernard.

Lilith smiled, cruelly, "Yes, exactly," Lilith said, nearly sneering at her, "I'm surprised that someone of your…intelligence knew that."

"Oh, I know more than you think," Giselle said, angrily,

"For example, I know that you want to force us to do something else that we do not wish to do."

Lilith smiled, "It is true that I have a chore for you," she purred, "Something that shouldn't be so difficult to accomplish."

"Nothing that you ask of us is easy," Bernard whispered, angrily, "I doubt that this will be either. You probably want us to kill them."

Lilith raised a brow and continued, "I don't want you to kill them... *both*," she said, slyly, "Ares, I want brought to me, when you find him."

"And what of Aphrodite?" Bernard asked, managing to keep his voice calm.

"Oh," Lilith said, and laughed, "Her, I want killed on sight and I want *you* to do it."

Bernard closed his eyes. Lilith laughed as she left as quickly as she came. Giselle pulled him close and shook her head. A tear trickled down his cheek.

"You must find her and hide her, Bernard," she whispered, "I won't allow for her to take your mother from you too."

Bernard nodded his head once before kissing her gently on her lips and leaving the room. Giselle watched after him, feeling turmoil fill her heart and tried to remind herself that everything would be over with soon. When it was, perhaps Lilith would meet her end.

****

Bridget Talbot's tears coursed down her beautiful, round cheeks. Her long blonde hair stuck to her face. She was seven years old, yet had been shoved into a dark, cold cell by her grandmother, Lilith. She had been there for days, maybe weeks, though she had been separated from her parents for longer than that and she had begun to wonder if she had been forgotten.

92.

She wondered about her parents. Where were they? Were they looking for her? She didn't doubt they were. They loved her. She had always known that. Her Grandmother had never loved her. She always knew that too.

When she took her, Bridget had been terrified. She realized she was in trouble. She also realized her grandmother would hurt her.

Still, when they first arrived, she hadn't harmed her at all. They lived in a house and she made sure that Bridget was taken care of in all the months that they lived there.

Then, she began to prepare for a trip. Bridget thought that she was taking her to her parents. Instead, she locked her inside the cold, dank cell with a guard standing outside.

She had cried constantly and finally someone did come to her. He was a person like her, not a vampire like the rest of her family. Still, he was not fully a man, but a boy almost grown but because he was much older than she was, it helped her to calm her fears.

She shivered but the cold didn't bother her nearly as much as being alone. Sobs were wracking her body, but the guard didn't seem moved enough to open the small slot in the door to allow even a little light to chase away her fears. She trembled as the shadows turned to horrible monsters before her. Panic rose higher and higher and then, she screamed.

The slot in the door opened only a few moments later and Bridget looked into her friend's eyes. They were beautiful and tanned in color, but what mattered most was that they were kind. They offered comfort in a terrifying world that her child's mind did not understand.

"Bridget, have you hurt yourself?" He asked with concern lacing his voice and she knew that he was truly worried for her.

He wasn't just pretending to keep her quiet.

"No," she whispered walking closer to the slit in the door, "But I want my momma and daddy."

"You'll see them soon, Sweetheart," he said and she tried to smile at him. He wasn't exactly lying. He was only hoping that what he said was true.

"Now, will you eat for me?" He asked pushing a plate of food through the slot.

"Stay with me?" She begged, terrified to be in the dark again.

The door opened and his dark form filled the doorway, "I'll stay as long as you need me to," he said softly.

She ate in silence. Bridget only felt a little better. The boy couldn't possibly understand the torture that she was going through. Still, questions floated through her seven year old mind. Where was her momma and daddy? Did they forget about her? Had they put her in the dark?

Even though she knew the answers to the questions, sometimes the panic made her doubt. Bridget lowered her head as tears fell down her cheeks. She was frightened and cast aside and wondered whether she would ever see her parents again.

Her friend grasped her hand and whispered to her, "I will protect you," he said so softly that it was nearly inaudible, "I promise that you will see your parents again."

She looked up into his face as hope lit in her child's heart. Slowly, she smiled for the first time in a very long while.

****

Thomas and Eliza pushed through the growth that snaked over the trails in the forest, finding the right path to the neighbor's field. His father had asked him to deliver a package to one of the neighbors on the other side of the neighborhood and he knew if he snaked through the outer part of the forest, it would take away at least five minutes of walking.

He was in a hurry. He wanted to get back sooner to see Marissa. He was worried about her. She had always been like a sister to him. Unfortunately, his father made him take Eliza with him and that slowed him down.

Thomas looked back at her, frustrated with her, not only because of her slow gait, but also because of the look of terror on her face. He realized where the fear came from and that annoyed him further. How could she put trust in their parents delusions?

"Eliza, come on," he said, fighting the need to pull her along.

"I don't want to go any further," she said, stopping and crossing her arms over her chest. Still, her eyes were wide with apprehension, "I want to go back."

He groaned as he stood in front of her. There was no one more stubborn than Eliza. Rarely did someone make her do something she did not want to do. Still, he would try.

"Don't tell me that you still believe this nonsense," he mocked, rolling his eyes. He walked over to her, shaking his head.

"I do," she said and raised her eyes to his. It surprised him to see that tears rested in their tanned depths, "You should too."

"Vampires are not real. You know that, don't you?" It took a great effort to hold her gaze when she was so sure of herself. Somehow, he managed.

Instead of answering him, she frowned. It looked as if she were about to say something, but then she just looked past him and asked, as if defeated, "How far until we're out of the forest?"

"About ten more minutes of walking," he said, surprised that she didn't argue and even more surprised that he seemed to be prevailing in an argument with her. Still, he hated that his parents had made her so frightened. He knew that he wouldn't be able to keep her within the forest for long without having to turn back around. He looked down the path and saw that the rest of the path to the field were clear. He smiled as an idea came to him. He raised his brows as he looked back at her, "It will only take five minutes of running."

She sighed, looking hesitant, "Well then, I guess I'll beat you in a race...again," Eliza finally said and a slow, hesitant grin lit her face. Thomas didn't give her time to change her mind. He turned and began to run.

His legs pumped hard but he still heard her behind him, and he tried to make his legs propel faster. He could feel the muscles in his legs and back stretching. His breaths became shallow as he pushed even further.

He hadn't been paying attention. He hadn't seen anything at all. He had been too focused on winning the race, when he slammed into something hard. He fell backwards with a terrified yelp.

A noise reached him and he realized that it was laughter and it did *not* come from Eliza. It was too soft to be hers, too musical.

He frowned as he realized that he had run into someone...not something. He looked up with an apology on his lips but stopped as he stared at the woman in front of him. She had beautiful, long hair that had blonde, brown and red streaming through it. Her face was round and stunning with wonderfully full lips and she was dressed extravagantly, but it was her eyes that held him mesmerized. He watched as her eyes shifted from green to brown and gasped.

She sniffed the air and then smiled and that's when he saw

them. Fangs sharp and deadly extended over her bottom lip. Thomas trembled.

My God, they were right, his mind screamed, *My parents were right!*

"You smell familiar," the vampiress said with a crooked grin, and then, nodded her chin behind him, "So does she. I've smelled your scent before."

Thomas closed his eyes for a moment, wishing that he listened, and knowing that he had condemned not only himself and Eliza, but his parents too. They wouldn't survive the deaths of all of their children.

"Thomas…" he heard Eliza whisper in warning. There wasn't a hint of her strong nature in her voice, only complete and utter terror.

He wanted to tell her to run. He wanted for her to survive but he couldn't say anything. Instead, he stared up at the vampiress stupidly unable to help himself or his beloved sister.

Thomas closed his eyes, praying for a miracle. When he opened them the woman just grinned at him, flashing her fangs and inciting another wave of horror. He backed away from her and realized that he could move once more. Slowly, he rose on trembling legs, but the vampiress still did not attack. Instead, it looked as if she were listening to something intently.

Then as if she had merely disappeared, she was gone. He looked around, but she was nowhere in sight. Eliza stood, trembling, a foot behind him. Tears streaked her face.

He walked to her, grasping her shoulders, "Are you alright?" He asked, but she didn't answer. Only another tremor of fear worked through her. Finally, he shouted, "Eliza, are you okay?"

Finally, she shook her head as she looked into Thomas'

eyes, "Do you believe Momma and Daddy now?"

"Why wouldn't I, after what I have just seen?" He asked and noticed that his voice still trembled.

Unexpectedly, Eliza began to cry and he held her close, "We've got to get home," he whispered. He felt her nod her head.

When they turned, he found a man standing on the path. He had blonde hair which shined almost white and light green eyes that sparkled. He was very muscular and his skin was sun kissed. He seemed perfectly normal but Thomas was still cautious.

"Don't worry," the man said in a pleasantly deep voice, "I saw the woman with you. When I came, she ran away. Did she hurt you?"

Thomas stared at the man for a moment, knowing that he wouldn't believe him if he told him the truth. Only minutes before, *he* hadn't believed his parents.

Slowly, he shook his head, "No. She didn't harm us. She only frightened us."

"Regardless, I will escort you to the edge of the forest," he said with a voice tinged in what sounded like a European accent. Thomas was grateful the moment the man offered.

"Did you hear what the man said, Eliza?" Thomas asked, softly, "He has offered to take us to the edge of the forest."

Slowly, Eliza lifted her head. The man allowed her to study him and Eliza nodded her head, seeming calmer instantly. She began to walk and Thomas followed her.

The remainder of the trip through the forest was silent. When they reached the edge, Thomas turned to the stranger.

"Thank you, Sir," Thomas said and forced himself to smile.

"It was my pleasure," the man said, politely but it seemed

98.
as if his attention turned once again toward the forest.

"What is your name so that I can tell my parents?" Thomas asked, still keeping Eliza close, "They'll want to thank you."

The man turned back to them and smiled but he still seemed distracted.

"I have to say that my name is a bit odd," The man said with one raised brow, "I was named after a Greek god....Ares."

"Well, Sir, strange or not, they'll want to thank you," Thomas said, gratefully.

The man nodded his head and turned to the forest. He looked over his shoulder and grinned, "It's truly not necessary," he said.

Thomas was about to argue, but he blinked. In that second, Ares had disappeared. Thomas trembled knowing that the vampiress had done the same thing. In one day, Thomas was sure that he met two vampires. Only one thought kept repeating itself in his mind.

I should have listened to my parents.

Chapter Eight
Complications

Ares stood within the center of the forest, canopied by the green leaves. Light filtered through them here and there creating small streams of light. Large pine, hickory and oak trees rose above him catching the wind that came from the mountains which surrounded Winchester.

Ares inhaled deeply, trying to find the scent which caused him to leave Thomas and Eliza so quickly. He frowned as he sorted through the smells. They assaulted him in quick array.

Wild onions tickled his nose quickly followed by the

smells of various animals and burning leaves. He could smell a slightly fishy odor as the wind whipped over the stream and hit him full force in the face.

There it was, the scent that he'd been looking for. It was slightly woodsy with the hint of blood. There was a sweetness beneath that, mixing into a most pleasant scent. It was a perfume of sorts. One that could cause death if the vampire attached to it wasn't so…humane. This vampire never drank the blood of the humans. He had been taught well. After all, Ares himself sired him.

Ares followed the scent and came upon him standing beside the stream. Anrique Dubois stood facing him. He was just as he remembered him. He stood tall with raven black hair that had once been long but he had cropped it short to seem more modern. His blue eyes stared out from his strong, handsome face. He possessed broad shoulders and he was as muscled as he had been when Ares changed him on a French battlefield in the early fourteen hundreds. He had been a knight then, but had been mortally wounded. Ares had not been able to allow him to die.

"Ares, what are you doing here?" Anrique asked breaking Ares' thoughts. He looked at Anrique noticing the confused expression on his face.

"I should ask the same thing," Ares said, walking to him and taking his hand, shaking it in a strong, firm grip.

"How have you been, My Friend?" Anrique asked in a deep, pleasant voice interlaced with a slight French accent.

"I don't even know how to answer that," Ares sighed, "It's too complicated."

Anrique's frown deepened, "Why is it complicated?"

Ares regarded him for a few moments as if he was trying to decide whether to tell him or not. He sighed after a moment and then answered, "My son is alive," he said and Anrique's eyes widened as understanding dawned within their sky bright depths.

"Athena changed him?" Anrique asked, shocked that the vampiress so set upon revenge had done such a thing.

"That's why I'm here," Ares said with a sigh.

"They're here?" Anrique asked as his eyes narrowed in concentration. Something was trying to make itself known to him but he did not understand what it was.

"They are," Ares replied, closing his eyes, "Of course, Athena goes by a different name now, as does Eros."

A worried glint crossed Anrique's eyes. When he spoke, he did so hesitantly, "Her name wouldn't be Lilith, would it?"

Ares frowned, "Yes, it is," he said, surprised that Anrique recognized her name. Then, he realized something else, "Where's Abigail?"

Anrique smiled at the mention of his beloved's name, "She's here," He said, softly, "She's staying with our family at a home on the other side of this forest. The family's name is Preston."

Ares recognized their name but a visit with family did not seem the reason for Anrique's appearance. Ares searched Anrique's eyes and then his mind, seeing the reason for Abigail's visit to Winchester. It shook him to his core to hear his son's name whispered with such hate attached to it. He saw everything but still he asked, "She's dreamed a prophecy, hasn't she?"

Anrique nodded his head once, "There will be a war here," He said, but a frown didn't mark his brow, only confidence, "And you'll be happy to know that Lilith *will* die at the conclusion of it."

Ares swallowed hard, wondering if their plans for Bernard were the same as they were for Lilith. He took a deep breath as prepared himself to plead for Bernard's safety. He looked at his friend, knowing that he had to proceed carefully.

"There are some other things that you should be aware of first," Ares said, frowning, "Lilith has lied to my son since she took him. He believed her to be his mother and she has forced him to do horrible things. The most recent the cruelest."

Compassion crossed Anrique's face as Ares knew that it would, "What is this horrible thing?"

"There is a girl who lives here, who looks just like my son's wife," Ares said, rubbing his hand over his eyes, "Her family is wealthy. Lilith has ordered him to court her so that she can get close enough to kill her and her family. My son's wife will take this girl's place as the only living heir. He has refused, but Lilith has found a way to force him."

"Which is?" Anrique asked, stepping closer to him.

"He has a daughter named Bridget," Ares said, careful not to say Bernard's name, "She's seven years old and Lilith has taken her."

"She's threatened to kill her?" Anrique asked, assuming the most logical thing.

"No, it's worse and definitely against our laws," Ares said, looking into his eyes.

Realization crossed Anrique's face and then, horror twisted his features, "She's going to change her?" He asked, disgusted.

"Yes, but I know where Bridget is and I'm hoping to retrieve her before my son is forced to harm the girl," he said, "However, if I can't retrieve her, he will have to change the girl he's charged to kill and we'll need somewhere to hide her. We have to make sure that Lilith believes her to be dead."

"I promise that we will help," Anrique said, quickly,

"You'll bring her to us. To stay with you would welcome her death and risk this innocent child to be changed."

Ares smiled a bit ashamed, "Perhaps there is one more thing that you must know because it may cause complications."

"Yes?" Anrique asked with a raised brow.

"My son is Bernard Talbot," he said as worry clenched his gut.

Anrique's brow darkened and his face became troubled, "Yes, that *is* a complication."

****

Marissa lay on her bed staring at the ceiling. It was good to be home but she was having trouble sleeping. Mostly because she wondered, since she could now see Nicolas when she was awake, would he still come to her in her dreams. If he didn't, would the nightmares return. The prospect of the nightmares caused her to be restless. She didn't want to return to the nights of terror.

The slight click of the door knob being turned caused her to turn towards it. She identified who would enter before the door opened. It was around midnight and only one person would dare to go against her mother's orders of rest… Karena.

She entered the room. Her hair was pulled back in a ponytail. She wore white silk night shirt and shorts. Her eyes were that strange, beautiful nearly yellow color and they glinted in the near darkness.

Karena grinned at her and Marissa felt her mouth stretch into a smile.

"Karena, you know mother told you to stay in bed," Marissa asked in a falsely sweet voice.

Karena laughed, "Of course," she said, amused, "Now, why would you think I'd listen to her? Besides, I missed you."

104.

      She came to her bed and sat down, "You scared me. Don't ever do that again," Karena said looking into her eyes.

      "I didn't mean to scare you," Marissa said as Karena watched her with a raised brow. She searched her face intensely and Marissa shifted nervously.

      "Well, I guess I forgive you," she said and sighed, rolling her eyes, "But at least you were rescued by some cute boys…or should I call them men?" Karena asked and then, looked at Marissa with a sly, knowing look upon her face, "You seem to like the one who isn't married."

      Marissa shifted uncomfortably but did not answer. However, the expression on her face must have given away her feelings.

      "Are you dating him secretly?" Karena asked with frustration lacing her voice, "Is that why you went into the forest?"

      Marissa looked directly into her eyes, "No, that is not why I went into the forest," She said, frowning, "It was a stupid….stupid mistake. I should never have done it."

      Marissa sighed, deciding to tell her the truth but only minimally, "Yes, I do like him," she sighed, "Truthfully, I believe that I dreamed of him before I had even laid eyes on him."

      Instead of looking shocked, Karena looked relieved, "I am glad that you like him and not Bernard," she whispered.

      Marissa's eyes widened surprised. She had been certain that Karena adored Bernard, "Why would you not like Bernard?"

      Karena looked as if in deep thought for a moment and then sighed, "Maybe it is because I don't trust that his feelings are true. Sometimes, when he looks at you, I see only friendship. Other times, it looks like guilt and it makes me worry."

      Marissa's frown deepened and she looked down at Karena

studying her. A worried crease *did* mark her brow. Finally, Marissa sighed again, "Well, it doesn't matter. I do not intend to ever date him."

"Marissa…" Karena hesitated and a look of fear crossed her face.

"What is it?" Marissa asked studying her.

"I've spoken to Eliza about Bernard," she said, biting her bottom lip, nervously.

That didn't surprise Marissa. Karena and Eliza had managed a bond closer than twins. They talked about everything.

"What did she say?" Marissa frowned. For a reason that she didn't understand, her heart had begun to pound hard in her chest.

"She said that he was a…monster," she said looking up at her sheepishly, "And I think that she meant it…literally."

Marissa swallowed as her heart began to beat even faster, "Why would she think that?"

"Thalia told her some things that he's done," Karena said, frowning, "I don't know what they were but it frightened Eliza."

Marissa was quiet for a moment as her thoughts ran rapid within her mind. Karena's face became worried, "I know that you probably think that I'm childish and more than a little stupid for believing her."

"No," Marissa said, quickly, thinking of Thalia's reaction to Bernard, "I don't."

"Well, I am glad that you don't think I'm childish," Karena said and Marissa smiled shaking her head.

"I never said that," she said, teasing, "But I don't think that you're stupid for believing Eliza."

Karena smiled up at her and she stretched and then groaned, "I probably should go back to my own bedroom," she whispered and grinned, "Before mother comes in here and beats me senseless."

"She wouldn't do that and you know it," Marissa said, forcing herself to smile.

"Well, let's not find out who is right," Karena said, kissing her cheek and then looking down at her, "Don't do anything like that again. I couldn't bear to lose my favorite sister."

"I won't," Marissa said and then added, "I promise."

Karena was satisfied and turned and went to the door, giving her a mischievous grin before disappearing through it. Marissa stared at the door, as her mind replayed the things that Karena had told her of Bernard. She sighed trying to push it from her mind, but she couldn't as she lay there within the dark. Finally, she found a solution. She would ask Thalia and she would make her tell her the truth.

Still, as she lay there a shiver worked through her as fear settled into her heart like a block of ice. She closed her eyes hearing one word echo within her mind. *Danger.*

Chapter Nine
Hard Decisions

Anrique's mind kept replaying the conversation he had
with Abigail the night before. When he spoke to her upon his
return, he did not expected to be told that she knew the girl which
Ares had spoken of. She had met her and she knew her
name…Marissa Dalene. The rest of what Abigail told him had
been even more surprising.

He almost laughed at the irony. Who would have
suspected that the same woman Bernard was charged to kill, was
the same woman Nicolas had fallen in love with? The fact that

she looked so much like Giselle only made the irony worse.

He frowned for a moment before his brow smoothed in his usual calm façade. Everything was complicated, even more so than he had originally believed. The only bright light in the whole mess was Abigail's vision.

Still, it didn't stop Anrique from having to face the Prestons and tell them the truth. Thankfully, he was sure only one of them would be almost impossible to sway. He had always known Nicolas to be nearly feral at just the thought of Bernard or Giselle. Still, the possibility that saving Marissa would help to persuade Nicolas to assist Bernard. Anrique could only hope that it would be that easy.

He paced the living room of the Preston's home barely seeing the opulent gold and white room. He wasn't nervous. He never was. Situations such as these always worked out. Still, it would be…difficult and he needed to plan what to say.

He looked out of the windows, realizing that dawn had not come but the sky was beginning to lighten. He sighed. It was time and he still did not know how to begin. He wished that he had more time but he could sense his wife and the Prestons walking to the living room. He sighed again, shrugging. He would just have to be as diplomatic as possible.

Elizabeth entered first, dressed to perfection in a lavender sundress. White sandals covered her small feet. Raven curls twisted down her back.

Abigail followed wearing her hair in the way that he preferred, loose and hanging in golden curls. She wore a green dress that had a empire waist line and fell loosely to her knees. He smiled lovingly at her as she crossed the room to stand next to him.

Frazier entered quietly, as always. He wore a black suit

with a tie of the exact shade of lavender as Elizabeth's dress.

Then, Nicolas came. His wavy hair was neatly combed but he wore his white shirt opened at the neck. It had yet to be tucked into his blue trousers. Still, he was washed and he grinned hugely at Anrique.

Anrique stood within the center of the room with Abigail, and everyone else sat within the white chairs that circled the room. Anrique glanced around the room at everyone but stopped to stare at Nicolas for a few seconds more than the others. Even though Nicolas still grinned at him, he realized that he would be trouble. Still, he understood why. After all, what lengths would he go to for Abigail?

He moved his gaze to Frazier, knowing that he would fare much better with him. Frazier stared at him with a knowing look in his eyes, "Is everything okay within the family?" Frazier asked, frowning in worry.

"Everything is well," Anrique said, "Though, I must warn you that the leaders of each of the families will arrive her within the next few days. They wish to speak to Abigail before deciding whether they should send for the rest."

"That's understandable," Frazier said, studying him. The frown still crossed his brow, "But there is something else, isn't there?"

"There is," Anrique said in his calm, pleasant voice, "Ares is here. I spoke to him before I came here last night."

"Your sire?" Frazier asked, surprised. Though the Prestons had known Anrique and Abigail for two centuries, they had never met the vampire who had changed Anrique However, they had heard plenty of stories about him.

"Yes," Anrique said, "Though he is here for a different reason than ours, a more…personal reason."

110.

"Which is?" Frazier asked.

"Do you remember what I told you about his son Eros?" Anrique looked at Frazier, awaiting some sign that he remembered the story. When there was no indication of the memory, Anrique turned to Elizabeth. Elizabeth always remembered things that others didn't.

"Athena kidnapped him, correct?" Elizabeth asked, hesitantly, looking from him to Abigail. Perhaps she was trying to figure out where his story would lead.

"Yes," Anrique said and frowned for a moment trying to figure out what to say next. Finally, he sighed, "He's found his son…here."

"He's a vampire?" Nicolas asked, and Anrique faced him. The grin left Nicolas' face and was replaced with a look of concern and concentration. Anrique nearly smiled because this was exactly what he had wanted. Nicolas was listening, instead of breaking into a fit of rage.

"Changed by Lilith," Anrique affirmed, and then said very quickly, "He's been with her the whole time."

"He's been with Lilith?" Elizabeth asked as her eyes narrowed. She was obviously trying to think of all of the vampires who accompanied Lilith. Anrique didn't want her to figure it out too soon. That would end any chances of gaining Nicolas' cooperation.

"She makes him do horrible things," he said, "The most horrible is the most recent."

Anrique looked at Abigail, giving her a silent warning with his eyes. He was never nervous during such times, but Abigail's soft heart may not handle an outburst as well as he and he didn't want an argument.

Finally, he spoke again, "You see Eros is married and they

have a daughter named Bridget," he said, intentionally not using Bernard's birth name, "Lilith has taken her and is threatening to change her if he doesn't do her latest biding."

Elizabeth began to twist her hands in front of her, "Bridget is still a child?"

"She's seven years old," Anrique said, his face showing the seriousness of the situation. He heard Elizabeth gasp at the child's age.

"Is there anything that we can do to help?" Frazier asked, concerned. It always amazed Anrique how quickly Frazier always did the right thing.

"There is," Anrique said, swallowed before he continued, "But I must tell you everything. Lilith's new chore for him concerns you. Eros is being forced to kill Marissa."

Nicolas rose to his feet and his eyes flashed. His temper simmered within every feature of his face. Anrique spoke quickly, "If Ares can't save Bridget in time and Eros' hand is forced, then he will change Marissa and bring her to me."

"Why change her?" Nicolas asked, barely holding his temper.

"Lilith will require proof. The smell of that much of her blood within his bloodstream will be enough," he said. Nicolas' face fell as his eyes closed in defeat. He let the silence stretch, looking away from Nicolas and into the inquisitive eyes of Elizabeth. She seemed confused and finally she spoke.

"How did Lilith receive Eros when Athena took him?" Elizabeth asked, frowning.

Anrique quickly went through his mind to make sure there was nothing else that he needed Nicolas calm for and then sighed in relief when he realized that there was nothing. His face took on a expression of concentration. He would need to remain calm among the flaring tempers.

"Because Lilith *is* Athena," he said and waited for someone to realize who Eros was. It took less time than he anticipated.

"And Eros is Bernard," Frazier said, without asking. He looked from Anrique to Nicolas warily.

"Yes," Anrique said, looking toward Nicolas. Already his face was turning red with anger.

"We will not help *him*," Nicolas growled, low in his throat.

"And you would let an innocent suffer?" Abigail asked stepping forward, "Marissa isn't the only one in danger. There *is* a little girl at stake."

"How do you know that he's telling you the truth?" Nicolas asked, "He could have lied to Ares."

"He's not lying," Abigail said, as irritation colored her tone "I've seen the little girl in a vision, as well as Bernard, his wife and Marissa. She pulls them to the side of good. Bernard does return our kindness. Bernard helps Marissa kill Lilith."

"Marissa?" Nicolas' anger seemed to fight for control over the surprise and fear.

"She kills Lilith and she's a *vampire* when she does it," Abigail said. She looked him straight in the eyes, "Our cooperation is not only Bridget's only hope but Marissa's. I suggest that you decide quickly what you're willing to do."

Nicolas' eyes widened and he shook his head. Abigail narrowed her eyes and said forcefully, "Choose now," she ordered.

Nicolas groaned as if in pain. Moments passed as everything ran through his mind. Finally, he looked back up at Abigail.

"If he harms her, I *will* kill him," Nicolas said, "However, to save the child and Marissa, I will overlook the things he's done…for now, but don't think that he won't ever pay."

"Then, until Bridget and Marissa are safe," Anrique said, cautiously, "I have your word that you won't harm him nor Giselle?"

Reluctantly, Nicolas nodded his head, "You have my word."

Anrique should have felt relief but as he looked into Nicolas' eyes, he wasn't sure if Nicolas would be able to stick to his decision. Anrique closed his eyes. Oh, yes…Nicolas was going to be trouble.

****

Aphrodite felt Bernard's presence even before she could see him. She smiled but as he got closer, his fear and anger swirled around her and her smile turned into a strained grimace. She frowned as worry knotted in her stomach. He seemed more apprehensive than usual and she realized that meant something clse had happened and it was something horrible.

She turned to face him as he stepped into the clearing in which she stood. She forced her smile to return, hoping to break some of the worry which marred his beautiful, familiar face but instead of comforting him, her smile seemed to cause him even greater pain.

"Mother," he said with such urgency that she felt the alarm immediately as it radiated from his body, "We must get you away from here… away from me."

Panic hit her at the thought of being away from her son. She swallowed as her blue eyes widened, "Why?" She asked with such desperation that tears burned her eyes.

"Lilith, why else?" He spat, disgusted, "She knows you're

here. She's ordered your death."

"I don't care," Aphrodite said, shaking her head, stubbornly, "I will not leave you."

"You must," he said with such need that Aphrodite studied him again, finally finding his thoughts.

"She's ordered *you* to do it," she said in a whisper. Pain shot through her as she looked upon her son's tortured face and he nodded his head in affirmation.

"I won't do it," he said as a tear coursed down his cheek. She knew that he was saying it to reassure her, "I can't."

She stepped in front of him, feeling every bit of his pain and guilt, and caressed his cheek, "I know that you won't."

"So, you see why you must hide," he said, opening his mind to her. All of his fears, he showed to her. The most disturbing, an image of little Bridget with fangs protruding over her lip. A strand of blood dripped from each fang, falling down her chin. She shivered, pushing the image away.

"I couldn't bear for that to happen to her," he whispered, "However, I can't bear to kill you either."

She closed her eyes, warring with the selfish need to be near her son and the intense need to save her granddaughter. Finally, she opened her eyes and caressed his cheek once again, "You won't have too," she said, and then, kissed him on the cheek. She looked into his eyes, "Promise to call for me if you need me."

"Of course, I will," he said as another tear fell, "I'll call for you…*if* or when this ends."

"I swear to you that it *will* end soon, Bernard," she said, "But I will go, for now. However, if you call for me, I will come back."

He looked pained as she turned to leave, "I want to be able

to know you," he whispered so low that she wasn't sure that she heard correctly.

She turned to him, seeing his look of desperation and longing, and smiled, lovingly, "You already do," she said, "You just don't know it yet. I love you, *My* son."

He closed his eyes as the words caressed him. A mother's love was something that he had never had. When he opened his eyes, she was gone. A giant hole ripped through his chest and he wondered if his pain would ever end. A sob broke from him, echoing within the clearing. In that moment, he was more alone than he had ever been. Anger pulsed through him as his sobs subsided. He looked through the darkness vowing that for once, Lilith would not win.

Chapter Ten
Secrets and Escapes

Nicolas sensed Marissa's closeness rising in intensity as he drove closer to her house. He turned down the driveway and immediately it loomed large and welcoming before him. A balcony protruded above the front door and wrapped around its wooden frame. Two rows of windows, perfectly straight, marked the two stories.

He smiled softly. Somehow, the house fit the Dalene family. Slowly, he narrowed his eyes as he concentrated on Marissa. He saw that she was waiting for him in the living room, walking around the room, touching the light grey upholstery of the chaise lounge near the window, before finally sitting upon it.

He smiled, *I'm here,* he projected and she gasped with wide eyes, wondering whether she had imagined his voice. *You are hearing me, Marissa,* he projected. Her eyes widened again but this time, she looked out of the window.

He parked in the front driveway and got out and waved at her. The front door opened as soon as his foot touched the first step of the massive porch which led to the front door. He found that Helena stood inside the door smiling kindly at him.

"I'm so glad that you've come to visit Marissa," Helena said, smiling widely, "She's been restless and I think that a visit from a friend will cheer her up."

"I was hoping we would go outside for a little while," he said, smiling charmingly. Hope lit her eyes.

"That would be wonderful," she said, still smiling but her blue grey eyes did darkened a moment later, "But I'm not sure that Marissa will accept the offer. She's refused to leave these walls since coming home from the hospital even though some time outdoors would be good for her."

"Maybe, I should listen to my mother," Marissa said, causing her mother to jump. She stepped from the doorway of the living room.

Marissa was beautiful as always in a white sleeveless shirt and blue jeans. Her hair was pulled back into a sleek ponytail highlighting her high cheekbones. Although she smiled, he saw that she seemed tired. Confusion and worry marked her eyes causing shadows to rest in them.

He drew his brows together in worry. Had she changed her mind about him? Pain shot through him at the thought. Instead of letting the thought consume him, he swept his arm out in invitation for her to lead. She smiled as she stepped in front of him and Helena patted his arm in thanks. She watched as they walked out of the front door.

Marissa didn't speak to him as they made their way to the entrance of the immense garden. Flowers of all kinds lay within it and statues had been placed here and there. When they reached the center, Nicolas looked back and found that they were out of view of the house. He turned to her and she looked up as if surprised.

"Marissa, I can tell that something is wrong," he said and it surprised him that his voice shook, "Do you not want me here?"

Surprise crossed her face, "Of course I want you here," she whispered, "Though I am a bit surprised to see you in the daylight."

He laughed, "Our aversion to daylight is a myth," he said, shaking his head.

"Oh," she blushed, "I guess a lot of things are myths."

"Yes, they are," he whispered.

"But you do drink blood," she stated almost plainly.

"Animal blood," he said, with a shrug, "Though there are some of our kind who do drink human blood."

"I noticed," she said and shifted uncomfortably, "But do you have to drink blood."

He raised his brows, "If I want my heart to continue beating…yes."

She tilted her head, "Your heart beats?"

He grinned as he turned to stand in front of her and grabbed her hand. He placed it gently over his chest. Her eyes widened as his heart thumped beneath her fingertips. She looked at him with her lips parted in surprise. He grinned as he leaned closer to her and inhaled her scent, closing his eyes as his lips moved closer to her. Finally, her mouth touched his. Instantly, She leaned into him sliding her arms around his shoulders, deepening the kiss. He wrapped his arms around her tiny waist, lovingly…possessively, knowing that this kiss was better than the kisses in the dreams. This was real.

A moan escaped him as he almost lost control but the kiss

continued. He was near the edge of his sanity and though he should have backed away, he didn't. Her tongue swept out to trace his lips and his stomach tightened as he let his mouth open to gently caress her tongue back with his. His fangs sharpened as she pushed past his lips. The fangs scraped against her tongue and her back stiffened as she pulled away and looked up into his eyes.

Both of them were breathless. Both stared at each other with guarded expressions. Questions burned in her eyes and something else smoldered within their depths.

"I apologize," he said, swallowing the lump in his throat.

She smiled crookedly, "I don't regret that you kissed me, Nicolas. I would never regret that."

"But you were frightened for a moment," he said raising his brows at her reaction to his fangs.

She shook her head, "You would never hurt me," she said and shrugged her shoulders, "It only shocked me. I hadn't expected for them to…appear."

He smiled showing his dimples and took her arm and led her to a stone bench, allowing her to sit down.

"So, what was bothering you?" He asked as he sat beside her.

She sighed as she looked at him, "It is something that my sister, Karena, said."

Relief would have washed over him, if it wasn't for her expression. He reached out and caressed her cheek. She leaned into his touch, but still looked into his eyes, "Is there anything that I can do?"

"You can answer a question," she said in a timid voice.

"Alright," He said nodding his head.

When she spoke she did so with a bit of trepidation, "Are

you familiar with any other vampires besides your family?" She asked almost as if she were embarrassed.

An ice cold lump settled into the pit of his stomach.

"Yes," he said, guarded, "Why?"

"My sister believes that a friend of mine is a monster. I couldn't help but think maybe he was a vampire but I've never known him to be anything but kind," She said and then bit her lip, "His name is Bernard Talbot."

Nicolas was quiet for a long time. Her face fell as she realized the reason, "Then you've heard of him?" She asked, closing her eyes.

Nicolas nodded his head, "He is the one who changed me and my family."

Marissa's eyes opened wide in shock. A frown crossed her brow and tears burned in her eyes.

"He changed you?" She asked in disbelief and he nodded his head again.

"I've known him for three hundred years," he said, looking around and pushing down his temper.

"W-why did he change you?" She asked as he laced his hand in hers. He stared down at their interlocked fingers trying to decide how to proceed.

He bit his bottom lip, nervously, and then sighed as he continued, "There was a girl named Giselle," he said, looking away, uncomfortably, "I believed myself in love with her. Now I realize that I was only in love with her beauty, but then, it was all consuming. It didn't matter that another suitor was interested in her."

"Bernard?" Marissa asked, but he heard jealousy lace her words. He closed his eyes. That had been his fear when he had mentioned Giselle.

Still, he answered her, "Yes," he said, tortured, "I didn't understand what was happening then. I didn't know what or who I was dealing with."

"You didn't realize he was a vampire," Marissa said and he heard that slight harshness in her tone again.

"No, I didn't," he said, looking down, "I asked her to marry me and she accepted. I thought that she loved me, but she only wanted my money."

He bit his lip and continued, "She was selfish and cruel. She wasn't like you," he said, and then reached up to caress Marissa's face with his free hand. He looked into her eyes, but he was surprised to see the expression there. Her eyes seemed hard and for a moment, she looked exactly like Giselle. He had to glance away to continue, "On the way to the chapel, we were attacked. Bernard attacked Elizabeth first. Perhaps, it was because she was more fragile than the rest of us, but Frazier and I came to protect her and I stupidly put Giselle behind me. I was trying to protect her too, but I didn't know that she had her own plans."

He released her hand afraid that he would crush it in his rage, "He drained Frazier next and faster than I had ever seen anyone move, Bernard had gripped me by the shirt. Giselle stepped forward, staring unafraid at Bernard and it shocked me."

"She just stared at him and asked him what he was and that's when he gave her a choice," he said, frowning, "She could come with him and be like him…a vampire. She could live forever, stay young forever or stay with me and die."

He looked at Marissa again and she seemed more herself, though a bit terrified, "Giselle looked at me and smiled the smile that I had fallen in love with and betrayed me with it. She looked at Bernard and said, 'I only wanted him for the comfortable life that he would give me, but it seems that you will offer me more.'

"I was heartbroken and utterly betrayed," He said as anger washed over him anew, "When Bernard began to drain me, I didn't even fight. Then, I saw him go to Elizabeth and Frazier, though I didn't see what he was doing. When he reached me, I knew. He pressed his gashing wrist to my mouth and I tasted the thing that tortures me now. The last thing that I remember is that he apologized. It was strange. Then, the blood lust came. I am just glad that I didn't kill a mortal within the first few days. I was crazy with the wanting but I don't want to frighten you with that. Thankfully, we realized that the blood of animals would sustain us before we became murderers.."

"Why didn't he kill you?" Marissa asked in a thick voice. He didn't judge the question. He had asked himself the same thing too many times.

"Perhaps, to torture me," he said, looking into her eyes, "Because it has until I found you. Only you can hurt me now."

He looked up into Marissa's eyes and was surprised to see anger burning within them. It shocked him as it hit him in waves.

"Marissa," he said, but didn't know what to say next. He had never seen Marissa angry but as he looked at her, he saw the fury burning in the depths of her blue green eyes.

"If Bernard did that to you, what is he planning to do to me?" She asked as her pale face turned a violent red.

His stomach turned as a tremble worked through him. He hadn't expected the question and he hated himself for a moment because the thought to lie to her crossed his mind. Marissa's eyes narrowed, catching the deceit on his face before he could act on it,

"You know what he plans, don't you?" Her voice was deadly calm and he managed to look back into her fiery gaze.

He bit his lip nervously, "I'm afraid it will frighten you," he said, finally.

She blanched, "I'm already frightened," she said as a tremble worked through her, "It couldn't get any worse.."

He closed his eyes and when he looked at Marissa, it seemed that her face didn't look so red. He shook his head, trying to figure out how to begin. Finally, it came to him, "Do you remember Abigail?"

Marissa looked at him confused, "I do," she said, smiling, "She tried to erase my memory, though I think that it was her way of being...protective."

"I didn't want her to do that," he said, looking a bit angry himself, "However, why I've mentioned her is because she's married to a vampire named Anrique."

"I haven't met him," Marissa said, frowning.

"No, but you will soon," Nicolas said with a look of concentration as he continued, "The vampire who changed *him* is named Ares. He lived in Greece during the time of the gods and goddesses. The Grecian people believed him to be the god that he shares his name with."

Marissa's mouth opened in shock, "The Greek gods and goddesses are vampires?"

He smiled sadly at her, "Yes, but they are *just* vampires. They were never gods and goddesses. The Grecians noticed something different about them. It was something that they couldn't explain. When they began to worship them, the vampires upon Olympus couldn't deny it without putting themselves in danger. Most of them didn't want to be worshipped."

"But there were stories," Marissa said, frowning, "About him. About all of them."

"And some of them were based in truth," Nicolas said,

softly. He looked at her and found all signs of anger gone. She only looked at him with rapt interest upon her face. He continued, "What stories do you remember of Ares?"

Marissa's face scrunched in concentration, "I remember a story of Aphrodite having an affair with him and they had a son, Eros," she said and then shrugged, "But that's all that I remember."

He nodded his head, "Ares' mate *is* Aphrodite, though she never had an affair. She's always been mated to Ares," he said and a sharp look came across his face, "Eros *is* their son."

He looked at Marissa to make sure that she was listening and then continued, "Have you ever heard of Athena?"

"The goddess of wisdom?" Marissa asked as she squinted her eyes, trying to remember.

"Yes," he said and took a deep breath before speaking again. He frowned as he remembered everything that Anrique told him that morning, "She was Aphrodite's friend or so she thought. Athena was betraying her the whole time because she was jealous and tried to make Ares her mate instead. It turned out that Athena was jealous of much more. She hated Aphrodite because she was the goddess of love and beauty but also because she had the love of a son. So, when it came to light that she was plotting against Aphrodite, she was cast out of Olympus."

"Was she ever allowed back?" Marissa asked, frowning.

"No," he said, "But she came back anyway but only once. She stole Eros from Aphrodite and Ares. It was her revenge."

When he looked at her, she looked confused. Her eyes rose to his as a light dawned in her eyes, "Vampires can have children?" She finally asked.

"Yes, but their children are not vampires," he said, softly, "They're mortal."

Marissa's face looked sympathetic, "Did they find their son before he died?"

"They searched for him until his mortal years were over," he said, sadly, "Then they began to look for Athena."

"Did they find her?" Marissa asked, enraptured.

"Yes," he said, closing his eyes for a moment, "Ares found her here, though she goes by Lilith now instead of Athena."

"She's here?" Marissa asked, terrified.

"Yes," he said, swallowing, "She's the one who attacked you."

Marissa's face paled. A tremble worked through her and Nicolas reached out to her wrapping his arms around her.

"Why did she attack me?" Marissa asked as another tremor shook her.

Nicolas felt a tightness in his chest as he held her. He knew that he couldn't answer her yet. Slowly, he spoke, "I have to tell you the rest," he said, holding Marissa tightly.

She looked up at him with wide eyes, "There's more?" She asked, terrified.

"Yes," he said, getting ready to break her heart, "There's more."

She looked at him with raw fear marring her face and he hated himself in that moment for what he was about to do. He felt as if he were about to cry for the first time in two centuries. When he spoke, his voice was hoarse.

"Ares found someone else when he found Lilith," he said and he watched as she frowned.

Panic marked her face as she asked, "Who?"

"He found Eros," he said, trying to hold her gaze, "He was changed by Lilith."

"Oh," Marissa said putting her hand to her chest,

surprised, "I'm sure that Ares is happy to be able to have his son again."

"His name has been changed too," Nicolas said, keeping his gaze locked on hers, "His name is Bernard Talbot."

The air whooshed from her, "B-Bernard," she whispered, unable to speak any louder.

Nicolas nodded his head, slowly, "He's believed that Lilith was his mother. She's forced him to do many evil things and she's forcing him to help her now. Marissa, Lilith has plans for you."

Marissa narrowed her eyes, "What are they planning to do to me?"

Nicolas bit his bottom lip then and continued, "Lilith wants you dead, and she wants Bernard to do it," he said, watching her pale even further, "But Bernard doesn't want to do it. He's being forced too, but since he's met Aphrodite and Ares, they've found another way, though I don't agree with it."

"You keep saying that he's being forced," Marissa said, recovering a bit, "How?"

"Lilith has taken Bernard and Giselle's seven year old daughter, Bridget," he said, tightening his arms around her protectively, "If he doesn't kill you, Lilith will change her."

Marissa's eyes widened and then she said something that he had not expected, "Poor Bernard."

Nicolas felt his stomach drop, "You pity him?"

"It's horrible what she's doing to him," she said, shaking her head.

"Horrible," he said, shaking his head in return, "I do admit that, but I don't trust him. He may have been forced to do everything else but he wasn't forced to do what he did to me and my family and I don't trust him with what he plans to do to you."

"What do you mean?" She asked, paling again, "I thought that he was trying *not* to kill me."

"We only know all of this because Ares has spoken to Anrique. Ares is going to retrieve Bridget. He knows where she is," Nicolas said and he watched Marissa's face relax. considerably, "However, it will take time. If he can't get to Bridget soon enough, Bernard will have to change you because it will give him enough of the scent of your blood to trick Lilith into thinking that he's killed you. So, if everything doesn't turn out, you won't die," he said with tears in his eyes, "You'll be a vampire…like me."

Marissa trembled so violently that she looked faint. Alarmed, his hands moved to her cheeks and turned her face up to his, "I swear to you that we are doing everything that we can to make sure that you aren't changed."

"Why me?" she cried, "Why did they choose me?"

He swallowed hard, "Before I tell you, I want you to understand that I love you. I do not love Giselle. Do you understand?"

She nodded, "I do understand."

He took a deep breath, "It's because you look exactly like Giselle."

"H-How?" Marissa asked in shock.

"I don't know," he said, softly. Her tears fell down her face and he leaned in to kiss her lightly on the lips, "I swear to you that I will die keeping you safe, if I must," he said, determined.

Marissa shook her head, "That frightens me even more," she said, in a trembling voice and then, she straightened and raised her chin, stubbornly, "I will be changed before you give your life."

128.

He held her close as his heart sank into his stomach. He realized that even with all of his strength, he couldn't protect her. Terror threatened to incapacitate him but he pushed it away thinking, *there has to be a way.*

****

The boy looked into the mirror in the room Lilith gave him. He had done this so many times within his eighteen years that he should have discovered the answers he searched for. The only things he was sure about were that his eyes were tanned in color. His skin was light and the shade of caramel and his hair was a mixture of black and copper. Also, he was a mortal surrounded by vampires. Only one mortal lived within the house besides him and that was the seven year old little girl named Bridget in the cellar.

Everything else he knew about himself was only an assumption caused by other people telling him what they believed to be true. Lilith called him by the name of Caben. Bernard called him by another name which felt more familiar...Seth, which is what he went by when Lilith wasn't around. Bernard told him he took him eighteen years before. Lilith told him it had been sixteen years. He trusted Bernard. Too much about his body told him Bernard told the truth. He could never be quite sure his assumptions were true, but he did discover that Bernard had been punished for telling him. He assumed Bernard wouldn't have bore such a punishment if he had not been telling the truth. The fact he had, always made the boy's stomach roll in guilt. Bernard and Giselle had always been kind to him and for them to suffer, made him angry. The only way to cool the anger had been by taking care of their child.

He turned from the mirror, looking at the door. It was time to go to Bridget. He had become used to the schedule of sitting in the dark with her. When he realized the little girl was Bernard and Giselle's daughter, he decided to take care of their daughter in return for their kindness. It surprised him when he realized he loved her as he would a sister and it pained him every time he had to leave her alone in the dark.

He walked to the door but didn't open it all the way when he heard the two vampire guards. It was strange. They never left her unguarded. Automatically, he put up the walls around his mind, like Bernard taught him. Their voices were clear as he listened to them through the barely visible crack in the door.

"We are to get the mortal child ready," the biggest out of the two said. His tanned muscles bulged beneath his shirt, stretching the fabric to the point of bursting. He wasn't only the largest vampire out of the two. He was the meanest.

The smaller vampire looked sympathetic for a moment and then looked at the other hopefully, "She's going back to her parents?"

"Yes," he said, coldly and the smaller vampire looked relieved. His partner smiled darkly, "Of course, she'll be changed first."

Seth closed his eyes as he watched them round a corner. Fear pierced him and he swallowed. He couldn't let them take Bridget to Lilith. He couldn't allow her to become a child monster. He wouldn't.

He made his way to the cellar finding it unguarded, as he suspected it would be. He took his key out and unlocked the door. Bridget looked up quickly and her eyes widened with gratitude.

"Bridget, I want you to tell me how your momma and Daddy look," he said, knowing that if she kept their images in her mind, then he would be able to get her out without the others knowing. It would block her thoughts as they escaped the house.

She frowned but she started to think, "My Daddy has hair like mine," she said as he walked her out of the cell door. She looked up at him, surprised.

"Does your Momma have the same kind of hair?" he asked, quickly.

They began to walk again and she finally tugged his shirt and he was afraid that she was thinking of what they were doing.

"My Momma's hair isn't like Daddy's," she said and he almost sagged in relief. He made his way to the cellar doors that led to the outside. He pushed them, raising just his head above the opening and looking left and then right before taking her hand and pulling her into the sunlight. She covered her eyes as the light hit her. She hadn't seen sunlight in weeks. Instead, of waiting for her eyes to adjust, he picked her up and ran with her into the crowded street, running until they reached another.

Finally he set her down and allowed her to walk. Their scent would mingle with others and they would be nearly impossible to find. Panic nearly drowned him as he looked around, finally finding the street that would lead him the home of a trucker he met a few years before.

"Where are we going?" Bridget asked, looking up at him with wide blue eyes. She didn't look afraid, only trusting and that created a determination in him that he didn't know that he had.

"I'm taking you to your Momma and Daddy," he said as he found the house.

The man opened the door on the first knock. He frowned down at the two of them. The man's dark eyes scanned them, confused.

"Seth?" He asked and it took the boy a moment to realize

that he had said the name that he preferred to go by, the name that he would go by from then on.

"Mr. Starks, I need your help," he said, looking down at Bridget and then back up at the man again, "I need to get this little girl back to her parents in Tennessee, but I have no money."

The desperation in Seth's face, caused the man's face to soften is sympathy.

"Come in," he said, softly, "Are you in trouble."

Seth nodded his head as he pulled Bridget into the house, "We both are," he said, softly, "The woman I stay with. She's...abusive to this little girl. She took her from her mother and father."

"Then, we should call the police," he said, frowning.

"We can't. They'll take her away from them and they're good parents," Seth said, panicked, "But I know where they are. It's a place called Winchester, Tennessee."

Mr. Starks narrowed his eyes as he looked at them and then, nodded his head, "I believe you. I can help you get a ride to Tennessee. Give me an hour and I'll have someone to take you. You can stay here and wash up until then."

"Thank you, thank you, Mr. Starks," he said, relieved as he walked into the house.

He grasped Bridget's hand and said, "Don't worry, Bridget. We'll get you to your Momma and Daddy."

She looked up at him with relief and hope on her little angel's face, "You're taking me home?"

He nodded, "You're going home, Bridget."

Chapter Eleven
The Past and Penance

Marissa sat at her vanity brushing her hair when her door opened. She frowned as she saw Thalia step through. Night had already fallen so she was surprised to see Thalia at her home so late.

"Thalia, is something wrong?" Marissa asked as a frown crossed her brow.

"No," Thalia whispered as she stepped behind Marissa and took the brush. She began to brush her hair as she had when she was a child, "I just need to talk to you."

"So late at night?" Marissa asked, looking in the mirror and into the reflection of Thalia's eyes.

"Yes," she said as she began to braid Marissa's hair.

"Well, it certainly sounds as if there is something wrong, Thalia," she said, allowing her to finish the braid before turning to face her. She stared up into Thalia's face searching it for an answer.

Thalia sighed as she sat on the bed beside the vanity, "I guess there is something wrong."

Marissa tilted her head and then, raised her brow, "What is it?"

Thalia swallowed visibly and Marissa noticed that tears rested in her eyes, "I think it's time that I tell you why I dislike Bernard so much."

Marissa nodded, "I think it's past time," she said, softly, "I want to know."

She shifted and then, looked into Marissa's eyes as if terrified, "Will you promise to try to believe me, no matter how outrageous this sounds."

Marissa nodded, "I think I already know something about it."

"What do you mean?" Thalia asked, frowning.

Marissa bit her lower lip, "It's something that Karena told me."

"What did she tell you?" Thalia asked in a thick voice.

Marissa's frown deepened and her stare was unwavering, "She said Eliza told her that Bernard was a monster. She said that you told Eliza some things that he had done."

Thalia jumped, causing her to lean further away from Marissa. Suddenly, she was afraid to tell her but Marissa grabbed her hand and her face turned pleading, "Please tell me," she begged, "I promise that I'll believe you."

Thalia shook her head and closed her eyes for a moment. She turned, looking at the quilt which covered the bed and took a deep breath before facing Marissa again. Marissa stared at her and Thalia realized that she was waiting for her to begin. She inhaled slowly before exhaling before she spoke.

"Have you ever been told about my life before I lived here?" Thalia asked, forcing her gaze to Marissa's face.

Marissa frowned and shook her head, "I only know that you are from Louisiana. You moved here before I was born."

"There is a reason I don't talk about my life there," Thalia said, "When I was there, a lot of horrible things happened, things that were unexplainable."

Marissa's brows didn't relax from the frown as she asked, "What type of things?"

Thalia swallowed, "People began to disappear. The first to disappear was a neighbor of my parents named Emily. She was a little older than me and married. She'd just had a baby. Her husband had fallen asleep in their living room so he wouldn't wake them up when he got home from work. When he woke up to the baby crying, he found her gone. He looked everywhere for her, but no one found her until three weeks later. She'd been completely drained of blood and her throat had been ripped out."

Marissa gasped and her eyebrows finally relaxed, "Oh!" she breathed, "That poor woman!" Marissa stared at her wide-eyed.

"There were others," Thalia said, "The next two were field hands. The foreman saw them there one moment and the next, they were gone. A police man found them two weeks later in the same condition as Emily."

"The police man found them," Marissa said, looking pale, "Didn't they do anything?"

Thalia scoffed, "As long as it wasn't their daughters or sons or wives, they didn't care," she said, angrily, "We were people from the projects. Then, babies began to disappear. They would be asleep next to their mothers and then, they would be gone. They never found them. "

Thalia swallowed her tears as she continued, determined to tell Marissa everything, "My family hadn't been touched. We thought that we were lucky," she said, closing her eyes, "It turned out that we were the least lucky of all."

"People in your family disappeared?" Marissa asked as she blinked, causing one of the tears to fall from her eye to make a slow trek down her cheek.

"Yes," Thalia said in a broken whisper, "The first was my father. He went to get something from his car. He didn't struggle or scream. He just vanished. We never found him. My mother died of a broken heart two months later."

"Oh, Thalia," Marissa said, reaching for her hand but Thalia moved. She refused to allow her to comfort her because if she did, she wouldn't finish, "It wasn't the end. I was pregnant and I had this beautiful little boy. He was so tiny and I had such a hard time delivering him. We named him Seth."

Thalia winced as her chest contracted as she said his name, "I had such a hard time giving birth to him and I was so tired when we came home from the hospital that I would lay him next to me so I could rest," she said, brokenly, "Someone picked him up. I assumed that it was William. William loved to hold him. A moment went by and I realized that something' was different," A sob broke from Thalia and she would have screamed in renewed grief if Marissa wasn't sitting in front of her. She took a deep breath. She looked at Marissa.

"I didn't hear singing. William always sang to him. I opened my eyes to find a man holding my baby. I though he was William's boss at first, but when the man turned, I found that I was wrong. He wasn't a man at all. He was a vampire. I saw his fangs and the blood dripping down his chin. William was on the floor. The vampire had attacked him. I began to plead for him to give me back my son, but he didn't. I began to fight for him, but the vampire looked into my eyes and told me to sleep. I couldn't help but to do that. When I woke, Seth was gone. The vampire had taken my son."

"Did you ever find him?" Marissa asked as a tremble traveled down her body.

Thalia shook her head, "I never thought I would see that vampire again either, but I have," Thalia said, looking into Marissa's eyes wearily.

"Bernard?" Marissa asked.

"Yes," Thalia said, "And he's after you, a child that I love as my own and I'm terrified that he will harm you. I'm even more terrified of that than you not believing me."

Thalia bowed her head and began to sob. With the relief that she experienced because Marissa knew, came the fear. Fear of what Marissa now thought of her. Fear of what Bernard intended to do to her.

"I do believe you," Marissa said, stopping herself before saying the truth. She wouldn't expose Nicolas and his family, especially now. Thalia would consider them to be like Bernard. Instead, she said, "You've never lied to me."

Thalia looked at her relieved, "Still, I worry," she said, "He wants you. I don't know why but he does."

Marissa's lips spread into a shaky smile, "It frightens me

too," she said, looking up at Thalia, "But I suppose that I will be alright as long as I continue to refuse his advances. Maybe his interest in me will fade completely."

Thalia looked at her with fear so palpable it saturated the air around her, "Just promise me that you'll be careful around him," she said.

"I will," Marissa said, looking up into Thalia's eyes, knowing that she couldn't possibly know how careful she would have to be. Thalia closed her eyes in relief that Marissa believed her. Marissa didn't experience relief at all. Instead, she felt fear. Would Bernard risk his daughter's life or would he choose to do as he was forced? If he did, Marissa feared that her fate would be just like Seth's.

****

The next morning, Thalia had been too engrossed in the beauty of the dawn as she walked down the paths to her vegetable garden. The sun was just rising, casting an orange glow over the mountains. She had just noticed that birds had begun their melodious singing. She leaned her head back toward the sun, enjoying the heat. She wasn't paying attention. She wasn't being her usual, cautious self.

She knew that part of the reason was that Marissa believed her. It had taken a large amount of worry from her. She didn't need to wonder whether Marissa would think she was insane. She would no longer have to worry that Marissa would not be careful around Bernard Talbot. For the first time, in a very long time, she could relax.

She inhaled deeply, relaxing as she slowly exhaled. She hadn't sensed the danger near. She had only felt serenity.

Still, It shouldn't have surprised her when it happened. She should have realized that darkness lurked everywhere even on the brightest of days. She should have known there was no calm within her life.

Still, she was surprised when she found a hand over her mouth and was pulled too quickly into the darkness…so quickly she knew that the one who had subdued her was not human.

"I'm not going to harm you," Bernard's voice whispered against her ear. His breath was hot against her cheek and his hand remained over her mouth, "I only need to speak to you."

Thalia didn't trust him. How could she? She knew what he was capable of. Her heart pounded as he slowly released her and she stepped away from him. She looked around, surprised to find herself at the entrance to the forest. It was nearly two hundred feet from where she had stood but it had only taken him seconds to pull her there. She thought for a moment about running but knew that she was too far away. She knew that whether she fought or not, her fate was already decided.

She swallowed and slowly looked back at him. She didn't expect what she saw. Bernard was standing with his hands out as if to steady her or to calm her. His face wasn't angry or monstrous but nearly human with grief.

She took another step back but this time in surprise. She had never thought Bernard could have such human emotions. After all, she knew him to be a monster.

"You're frightened," he said, closing his eyes for a moment. When he opened them, she saw his sadness, "I suppose I understand. I should. You've only seen me as a monster."

Thalia stared at him stunned. Even if she had decided to run, she didn't think she would be able to convince her legs to move. She was not only too frightened but shocked. She had expected him to attack her, but instead he was speaking to her calmly and made no threatening move toward her.

"W-what do you want?" She stammered as suspicion wrapped around her like a blanket. She was sure that if she didn't find out his motives soon, she would die from the sheer confusion of it all, saving him the trouble of doing the deed himself.

"I want to make it right," he said. Instantly, she knew what he was speaking of. He was talking about Seth. Her heart trembled and tears formed in her eyes.

She shook her head, "There isn't a way to make it right, Bernard," she said, angrily, "You've taken my son from me. There is no way to take that back. You can't take back death."

"But I didn't kill him," Bernard said. His eyes pierced hers.

Thalia's heart nearly stopped. She stared at him about to accuse him of lying but something in his face and his eyes made her believe him. She felt stupid and naïve for doing so, but she did.

"He's alive?" She asked. He nodded his head, keeping his eyes on her as he took a step forward.

"He has the same skin color as you. He also has your eyes and hair," he said, hoping the description would convince her further.

"He isn't a v-."

"A vampire?" He asked and she nodded her head. Slowly, he answered, "No."

Thalia swallowed again. Hope sprang up in her chest, but she wouldn't allow it. Bernard could be lying. In all probability, he was. She shook her head again.

"I'm telling the truth," he said, but still, his voice wasn't angry but pleading. Again, she wondered if he was.

140.

"H-How are you going to make this right?" She asked with wide eyes. She shook her head again, pushing the hope away but her mind and heart betrayed her instantly.

What if *he's telling the truth,* she thought.

"I know where he is," he said and then bit his bottom lip for a moment before going on, "I'm going to get him and give him back to you."

Finally, a logical thought came to her mind. It screamed over and over in her conscience until she looked up at him with narrowed eyes.

"Why do you *want* to make this right?" She asked, suspiciously. Perhaps, he wanted to calm her so she wouldn't prevent his dark deeds to Marissa.

Bernard sighed and took a step forward. When Thalia cringed away from him, he looked at her apologetically and took a step back.

"I have recently learned that things aren't what I have always believed them to be," he said and immense pain crossed his face.

"What do you mean?" Thalia frowned as she swallowed over an odd lump in her throat.

"When I was a baby, a vampiress named Lilith, stole *me* from my parents," he said, biting his bottom lip before continuing, "I thought that she was my mother but she stole me for revenge. She's the one who changed me."

Thalia raised her hand to her chest as she listened. He frowned at her reaction and then continued, "I didn't know that she wasn't my mother until recently but I did know that she was always cruel to me. She's the one who made me take your son. I've always hated that I did that but it was part of her lessons."

"Lessons?" Thalia asked, confused.

"She said that I held onto mortal emotions," he said, angrily, "She's always been angry that I've taken blood but never killed but she allowed your son to live, since I did what she wanted. However, I do believe that she means to change him. That's what she's done to the other children. Seth has been safe this long because of me."

"Y-You know his name?" She asked as a tear fell down her cheek.

"Lilith calls him Caben, but I've told him his true name," he said, frowning, "I used to go back to your house and I would hear you crying out his name. It used to torture me but I believed that I deserved it. It was my punishment to myself."

"It wasn't enough," she said as a tear slid down her cheek.

"I understand that. I hope it helps you to know that Lilith's torture was worse," he said, "She still continues to torture me with her lessons. There have been so many of them."

"What kind of lessons?" Thalia asked, dazed.

He looked down and when he looked back at her, he had pure anguish on his face. He hesitated for a moment and then, his shoulders slumped forward in resignation.

"She told me that I have to kill Marissa," he said, feeling pain at the words, "When I refused, she took my seven year old daughter, Bridget and is threatening to change her if I don't."

Thalia gasped, terrified, "But you can't kill Marissa!"

"I'm not. My real parents are helping me," he said, calmly, "They're going to get Bridget so that I won't have to."

Relief flooded through Thalia, "So, you won't kill her?"

"No," Bernard said, unable to tell her the rest. Her relief was too great and he didn't have the heart to take that from her, "But I need to act as if nothing is wrong until I receive Bridget. Then, I'll go and get Seth."

142.

Thalia stared at him for a moment as her stomach turned. She had already told Marissa what Bernard had done. She didn't know if she would be able to undo anything, but she would try. She looked back at Bernard. "I will try to be kinder, but I won't tell Marissa to date you," she said, "I hope that you understand why."

"You don't have to," he said and sighed, "Act as you always have. I'm not doing this to get anything in return. I'm doing this to make it right. That's it. I only wanted you to know to expect it."

She nodded her head, knowing that the conversation had ended. She turned to walk away, but heard Bernard one more time, "Thalia, I hope that you know, how very sorry that I am."

When she turned, he had vanished. She frowned, knowing that she would either know the joy of her son's return or she would condemn herself to destruction. Either way, she knew that she had already begun to hope.

Chapter Twelve
Prophecies and Confrontations

Lilith stared out of the window of her bedroom with narrowed eyes. Blood was fresh upon her lips as fear trembled within her heart. It was an emotion she had not experienced often within her long, long life. It was one she *never* wished to feel.

As she stood there, the door opened behind her. She didn't turn. It was only one of her devotees and they wouldn't expect her to. They didn't deserve her presence and they deserved her gaze even less.

144.

     Lilith inhaled deeply and smiled. This devotee was newly changed, a female. She had been the daughter of a homeless woman, taken when she was just a baby. However, this one was special. She had visions.

     "What is it that you want, Mari?" Lilith asked and the girl stepped closer.

     "I've dreamed," She said, softly and Lilith turned to her, raising her brow.

     When she looked into the girls face, fear settled further into her heart. Mari looked apprehensive. That meant something was wrong. She stepped closer to her.

     "What is it that you've dreamed?" Lilith asked, putting kindness into her voice for the girl. Mari was one of the few immortals she showed kindness to. After all, the girl had a purpose that suited her. She kept Lilith alive.

     "Bridget has escaped," The girl whispered.

     Lilith narrowed her eyes and nearly laughed, "You're mistaken," she said, smiling, "That's imposs-."

     "But I'm not, Ma'am," Mari interrupted, lowering her eyes, "She's with Caben, though he's going by Seth now."

     "And you've just dreamed this?" Lilith asked, angrily. The girl cringed and Lilith softened her voice, "I'm not angry with you, Mari. I'm angry with the one's who were in charge of her."

     Mari straightened and sighed as if in relief, "I've just dreamed it," she said in a small voice, "Just before I came to you."

     "That's very good," she said, patting the girl's shoulder, "Do you know where they are going?"

     "Yes, Ma'am," she said, licking her full lips, "They are in a truck. Caben intends to deliver Bridget to your son and his wife here."

A slow smile came to her face, "You've done very well, Mari."

Mari looked at her, concerned and Lilith caressed the girl's cheek, "Don't worry, My Dear," Lilith said, lovingly, "I know what to do."

****

Marissa stood within the parlor as fear nearly suffocated her. She looked out of the window, wondering how her perfect life had taken such a turn. Once, she had been able to enjoy the sunlight without fear that she would die. Once, she had no danger around her.

Perhaps, it's always been there. I was just blind to it.

"Marissa," Her spine stiffened at the sound of Bernard's voice. She closed her eyes and tried to calm her heart before she turned. Slowly, she exhaled the breath she didn't realized she had been holding and turned to face him.

He frowned as he looked into her eyes, "You look frightened."

"Shouldn't I be?" She asked and she was surprised to feel another emotion come to the surface.

She was hurt. She had always viewed him as a friend and he never cared for her at all. She *had* cared for him though. She worried for his feelings when she believed he was in love in with her. She cared when she thought she hurt him. All of that care was for nothing. It hadn't mattered.

He stepped closer as his expression became pained, "You know?"

"You thought Nicolas wouldn't tell me?" She asked, biting her bottom lip, "Or Thalia?"

"Nicolas?" He asked. He pursed his lips as his eyes

darkened, "So, you *are* connected to him?"

Marissa nodded her head, "For a while now," She said, frowning, "I'm in love with him. Of course, it sounds like you already knew that I was with him."

"I wasn't sure," Bernard said thinking of Nicolas' attack on Giselle, "But I did know that he was interested in you."

"So, you must have known he would tell me and you should have known Thalia eventually would," she said as anger rose in her chest.

"I realized they would," he said and cautiously stepped forward. She didn't flinch or back away. It troubled him that she seemed so calm. He studied her for a moment before leaning forward and putting his hand over his face, rubbing it across his eyes, before looking back at her.

"And still, you came," she said, frowning. He shrugged and her temper hit her.

"I-I didn't realize you found out," he said, looking at her so forlorn that her heart clenched, "I was aware of Nicolas' connection to you but not yours to him. Thalia may have been too frightened to tell you. I had no reason to know that things would have changed, but I would have come anyway."

"Why?" She asked, walking a little closer to him, "Why would you come here?"

"Because I would want to know that you understood what had happened," Bernard said and then sighed, "Marissa, it is true that I am not in love with you," he said, "Though, I'm sure that gives you more relief than hurt. However, I have always thought of you as one of my dearest friends."

Marissa scoffed, "Even when you were planning to kill me?" She asked, angrily.

Bernard stared at her for a moment as hurt swept over his

face. Finally, he spoke very slowly as if each word were painful, "I never meant to…kill you," He said, shaking his head, "Ever since, the order was given to me, I've tried to find a way…not to."

"You've done evil things, Bernard," Marissa narrowed her eyes, "Are you saying that you were trying to abstain for those also."

"Not from what I did to Nicolas and his family," he said as guilt marred his features, "I let my…temper and jealousy rule but I was forced to do what I did to Thalia. That I am trying to rectify."

"You killed her son!" She nearly screamed.

"No, I did not," he whispered, "He lives and he will be reunited with her soon."

Marissa looked at him skeptically. She raised her brow and then sighed.

"Marissa," he said as calmly as he could, "Don't you understand why I've done everything that I've done to you."

Marissa's face fell and she closed her eyes, "Yes," she breathed, looking at him sorrowfully, "I do know why…Your little girl does need to be saved but I'm afraid of what will happen to me."

"We're trying to make sure that won't happen," he said, standing and going to her, "I promise you that we are."

"And I should accept your promises, Bernard?" She asked, looking up at him.

"You should, because I do care for you," he said, pleading, "Please believe me."

She looked up at him and for a moment, she could see the truth in what he was saying. A lump rose in her throat.

"What if you have to change me?" She asked with wide eyes.

"I will tell you as soon as I find out," he said, gazing down at her, "But I don't want that to happen either. However, I know that it is better than you ceasing to exist. I couldn't bear that. You are the only friend I have ever had. You truly cared about me before you realized what I was."

Marissa's heart trembled and tears came to her eyes, "Although I am angry and hurt, I truly care about you now," she said and then sighed, "And I care about your child. I wouldn't put her in danger, even if it cost me my life but I do think I have a right to be scared."

"I promise you that your life will not cease for my sins," he said, taking her hand in his, "I won't allow that to happen."

She shook her head and looked up into his eyes. Tears welled in their depths, "Then, I suppose that my life is in your hands, Bernard," she said as a tremble shook her, "And I will have to trust that you will do as you say."

Marissa closed her eyes as a tremble shook her. A tear released from her eye as she worried that her trust may get her killed.

****

Ares was grateful. Everything had fallen into place as he made his way to New York. He did not even have to call for assistance. He found help as he crossed into the Kentucky border. That help was the leader of the Italian family, Dominic Minaci.

Dominic was a vampire of old. He had lived nearly five thousand years but looked only eighteen. His black hair was combed back from his boyishly handsome face revealing dark olive skin and eyes the color of mahogany, fringed in long, thick lashes. He had a short wide nose with full lips that revealed deep dimples when he smiled. He was tall and well muscled and had strength that surpassed Ares by ten. However, he rarely had to use that strength because he emanated boyish charm and people and vampires alike saw only honesty in his face.

They reached New York fairly quickly, but as they neared the house that Lilith owned, Dominic grasped Ares' arm. He looked at him, confused sensing the first hint of trouble.

"Are you sure that she's here?" Dominic asked in a deep Italian accent.

"I saw her," He said confused.

Dominic interrupted, "But listen," he said, looking at him with wide eyes, "There's no heartbeat within."

"She *was* here," Ares insisted, feeling his heart drop, "I know that she was."

"Don't worry, Ares. We can still go in there," Dominic said and smiled, reassuringly, "If she has been moved, we can convince them to tell us where she is."

Ares frowned and then nodded his head, "I have to find her," he said with a tremble in his voice, "I won't go back to my son without her."

Dominic looked at him sympathetically, "Don't worry, Ares," he said and smiled, "I will do what you need done. Besides, I never back down from a fight. They're too much fun."

Dominic looked toward the house, concentrating very hard, "Two vampires are within," he said and inhaled, "They are younger than both you and I. I don't sense any others, but these seem nervous. Unfortunately, it won't be much of a fight but still, it is a fight."

Dominic grinned and moved to the front door. Ares' neck prickled in alarm, "What are you doing?"

"What better way to get attention than to go through the front door," Dominic asked. His grin stretched across his boyish face as he raised his large booted foot and kicked the door in, causing it to splinter in every direction.

Ares stepped behind him and followed him through the door. No one was about within the entryway but Dominic pointed up the stairwell. A moment later a young vampire with copper colored skin raced toward them. Dominic's fist shot out, hitting the fledgling in the jaw so hard that he slid across the floor, hitting a wall. Ares watched as Dominic picked the young vampire up by his shirt, sliding him up and knocking pictures from their nails as he did.

"Stop fighting," Dominic ordered but the fledgling only kicked harder resulting in another blow to the jaw from Dominic.

Ares was staring at them but a moment later Dominic's back stiffened.

"Ares the second one," he said, tilting his head toward the stairwell.

It was too late. A blow to the face caused Ares to turn. He frowned at his attacker. This vampire was largely muscled but those muscles did not assist him at all. It hadn't even caused Ares to flinch.

This stupid imbecile still thinks his muscles mean something, Ares shook his head.

The fledgling's second blow hit him in the stomach. The fledgling's eyes widened as surprise flooded his face when Ares didn't move. Ares' patience finally gave out and he grabbed the fledgling by the throat slamming him against the wall so hard that it cracked from ceiling to floor and caused a deep impression in the plaster in the shape of his body. The stupid vampire began to fight only stopping when Ares shook his head ominously and gave him a threatening look.

"Hello, Gentlemen," Dominic said in a falsely sweet voice. He cocked his brows and grinned, "We need for you to answer some questions. If you don't, I'm sure that my friend will gladly tear each limb from your body with a smile upon his face."

"W-who are y-you?" The smaller vampire gasped.

Dominic narrowed his eyes, "Perhaps, you should know the names of the vampires who can, most willingly, take your life," he said with a crooked grin, "My name is Dominic and this is Ares."

"A-Ares," The small one said, struggling. He had obviously heard that the Greek gods and goddesses had really been vampires.

Dominic raised one long, thin brow. He knew that the vampire was calculating his age and Dominic laughed, "Oh, yes. You are in trouble because he's old but…I'm older," He grinned, "That means that we are much stronger than you and much more capable of giving you great pain."

The vampire trembled beneath Dominic, "Now," Dominic said, menacingly, "You do have a choice. It's very simple. Do you want to continue to breathe or not?"

"Breathe," the young one gasped.

"Good," Dominic said with a grin, "Now…there was a little girl here. Where is she?"

"W-we don't know," The vampire said and then, quickly continued when he seen the evil glint in Dominic's eyes, "We were supposed to prepare her. Lilith was going to change her before her son realized what had happened. A mortal took her before that could happen. Caben is his name."

Dominic laughed, "A *mortal* stole the child from you."

Dominic shot Ares a look and then, looked at the vampire, "Open your mind to me," he said, "It's the only way that we will know that you tell the truth."

The vampire immediately released his mind to Dominic

and he saw the few images of Bridget and of Caben but then there was the memory of the empty cell. Dominic blinked and then looked at the vampire.

"Is there anything of Caben's here?" Dominic asked.

The vampire pointed with a shaking finger at a rack with coats hanging from it, "The brown one is his," He said and Dominic released him to retrieve it. The smell of earth reached Dominic as he moved back to the vampire that was rubbing his throat. He looked at the vampire.

"I have some advice for you and your friend," he said, raising both brows, "It would do you some good to realize that this family may not be the best one for you. Also, you might want to hide. Lilith doesn't treat anyone who fails her well. Usually, they end up dead."

Ares still had the large vampire by the throat and Dominic touched his shoulder, "I'm sure that he'll behave if you let him go, Ares," Dominic said, "We have all that we need."

Ares let the other vampire go and followed Dominic out of the door. Neither vampire bothered to attack.

"What are you doing?" Ares asked, frowning.

Dominic held up the coat, "Caben's scent is on this," he said, smiling, "We can follow it to find him and your granddaughter."

Ares nodded his head, feeling relief that the boy had taken his granddaughter, saving her from Lilith's evil deed, but he knew that they must find her and the boy before Lilith found them because if she did, all hope would be lost.

Chapter Thirteen
Kindness in Darkness

Seth looked down at Bridget as yet another stop brought them to yet another town. They were in Ohio near the Kentucky border. Seth did not know the exact town. He only knew that he feared the delay and he wondered if he would be able to put Bridget back into her parents arms before they were found.

He didn't want to think about what would happen if they were found. He shivered as he imagined his fate and shivered again as he imagined Bridget's. He had witnessed what had happened to the ones who had betrayed Lilith. They had all perished in the most torturous of ways. She would view his punishment as an example to anyone else who dared to deceive her. He swallowed hard as dread pumped through him with each beat of his heart.

"Get a place to sleep tonight," the trucker said. Seth's eyes widened and a tremble shook him. He couldn't risk sleeping in the truck and no hotel would accept him when he had no money.

"Sir, I thought that we would be going straight through," Seth said, looking at Bridget's sleeping face. The trucker frowned, really seeing Seth for the first time. He noticed that the boy looked panicked. Seth quickly spoke again, "She wanted to be back with her momma and daddy soon."

The coachman looked down at Bridget and sighed, regretfully, "I'm sorry, Son," he said, frowning, "But it's against regulations for us to drive any further," The man's frown deepened yet again and distress filled his face, "Do you need help finding a place to rest for the night?"

Seth bit his lip wondering whether to tell the man or not. He had learned to trust few in his short life but there was something about this man that seemed kind. Seth nodded his head, "I do," he said with wide eyes, "We don't have any money."

The coachman looked at Bridget again and his brown eyes softened further. He took off his ball cap and ran one hand through a thick mass of brown hair. It seemed as if he was trying to decide what to do. Finally, he looked at Seth and sighed, deciding in a moment. Still, his face looked fretful as he gazed at him.

"I have a place for you to stay," he said, smiling embarrassed, "Though you can't come out of your room while there."

Seth frowned up at the man, "Why is that, Sir?" Seth asked, suspiciously.

"It's a brothel, Son," he said, "But I'll be there. The madam, Miss Kimela is kind though and she won't let nobody mess with you."

Seth swallowed and looked out of the window. He realized that it was better than sleeping in the streets and waiting for the vampires to find him and kill him. He nodded his head and picked up Bridget to follow after the trucker.

They walked up the street a short way and around the back of what looked to be a normal house. A window opened as they passed beneath it.

"Charles," One of the women called. Seth saw her and was surprised to find that she was pretty with long dark hair, "Are you coming to see me?"

He laughed, "I am, Nora," he called back, "But I must speak to Miss Kimela first."

The girl smiled, "I'll see you soon, then," she said in a seductive way that made Seth raise a brow at it's implications.

Charles walked through the double doors and bid Seth to follow. He frowned at the man wondering if he would be allowed.

"This is a brothel, Son," the man said with a grin, "But that doesn't mean that they are bad people. They'll make sure that you stay safe."

Seth nodded his head and stepped through. It was a large square room with couches and chaise lounges covered in bright red upholstery scattered about the room. Men sat on them, some with women upon their laps. None of them paid any attention to Seth or Bridget.

156.

Then, Charles pointed and smiled, "There she is," he said. Admiration showed on the man's face which surprised Seth. He had never seen anyone show any type of respect for women such as these.

Miss Kimela stood in the corner, observing her girls. She was a large woman, but beautiful. She had a massive amount of strawberry blonde hair which flowed down her back. Her eyes were a hazel color and they twinkled with merriment or mischievousness. Her cheeks were darkly rouged as was her full lips. She wore a long flowing, red gown and although she was more clothed than any other woman in the room, she certainly wasn't more modest for her breasts nearly popped out of her gown.

She saw Charles and grinned, walking toward him. She stopped short when she saw Seth and Bridget and looked at him with a raised brow.

"They didn't have anywhere to go for the night," Charles said, sheepishly, "I couldn't leave them in the truck or on the streets."

Miss Kimela smiled, widely, "Why, Charles," she said in a country drawl, "You know that I wouldn't turn away anyone in need."

She frowned as she looked at Seth, "I have a room for you and the little one, but do you know the rules?"

"Yes, Ma'am," Seth said, "I promise to stay in the room all night."

Kimela patted Seth's shoulder, "Good," she said, raising her brow, "I wouldn't want to ruin you…yet."

She turned and Seth followed her, "I will pay you," he said, quickly, "I can send you the money when I get to Tennessee."

Kimela laughed, loudly, "There's no need for that," she said, "I've enough money. Just stick to the rules."

Seth nodded his head as she led him up the stairs and to the very back of the building. No one came back the way she led them. Finally, she stopped at a door and opened it. There were two beds inside and there was a door which led to a small bathroom.

Kimela raised her brows, "Is this good enough?"

"Yes, Ma'am," he said, relieved, "Thank you."

She nodded her head once, "I'll bring you some supper at around six," she said and patted Seth's shoulder, "And don't worry. Nobody will bother you. Get you some sleep."

Seth smiled as both Miss Kimela and Charles exited the room. He gently lay Bridget upon one of the beds and then, laid down on the other. He closed his eyes thinking that perhaps, he would have a little nap.

****

Elizabeth felt her heart tremble as she looked around her living room. She held out hope that the family would not come and there would be no war, but they had and all of her hopes had been dashed. As much as she loved them all, they represented her loved ones who could die.

She looked toward the Greeks. Callista Christos stood as a goddess among women with her long wheat colored hair that shined like silk. Her eyes were sea green and her skin was beautiful and tanned. She wore a long white gown that hugged her every curve. At one time, she had been called Gaia, the Greeks version of Mother Earth.

Beside her stood a man who was just as impressive. Nico Drakos was as tall as Frazier but thickly muscled. He possessed hair that was raven in color and his eyes were a deep blue. He had been thought to be Uranus. Both he and Callista hated that they were thought of as those mythical deities and they changed their names as soon as the beliefs in the myths had faded.

Standing near the fireplace was Pheonix and Hazel MacLeod, the heads of the Scottish family. Pheonix was a handsome man. He was about six feet tall. His face was boyish and he owned a head of dark hair. His eyes were light brown and were kind and inquisitive. He possessed wide shoulders and arms which were strong in appearance and tapered down to an abdomen rippling with lean muscle. He stood near his wife, flanking her protectively.

Hazel was a woman of beauty with silky blond and brown locks. She was tall and exuded great authority. She had a wonderful hourglass figure that made the other men in the room look at her with favor and the women with slight jealousy but she smiled shyly diminishing their envy quickly. She barely looked at anyone for a long period of time except for her husband.

On the other side of the room were Briana O'Dear and Ryan Sullivan, the heads of the Irish family. Briana's hair was red as was Ryan's but hers was long and waved down her back. Her skin was pale and covered with many freckles. She had beautiful green eyes that shined from her stunning oval face and lips that seemed in a constant pout. She was small in stature but stood with regality that made people listen to anything that she said. She raised her chin and looked toward Abigail as her green eyes bore into the woman.

Ryan was a man of a powerful build though he was not as tall as most. His hair was a deeper shade of red than Briana's but his eyes were the same shade green. His skin was flawless and pale within his round, young face. He possessed a strong nature about him and had a stubborn tilt to his chin. His short stature did not take away from his strong appearance. His body was thickly muscled, making him seem taller than he actually was.

In the center of the room was Abigail. She retold the vision and each looked at her with an expectation that rose around them like a cloak. No one spoke for a long time and for a moment, Elizabeth believed that they would refuse to fight. Finally, Callista stepped forward and Elizabeth knew that all hope was lost.

"It seems that you need assistance," she said and a small smile came to her face as she looked toward Nico. He shook his head, "You shall have it within our family."

Abigail looked around the room, "Is there anyone else?" She asked, looking at each of them in turn. When no one else answered, she raised her brow, "Do you not want peace? As long as Lilith lives we will not have it."

Elizabeth watched as Hazel leaned to whisper in her husband's ear. He smiled as he caressed her cheek, "Are ye sure?" He mouthed to her and she nodded her head. He released her and stepped forward.

"Ye have us," Pheonix said in a deep voice.

Abigail smiled, crookedly as she looked at Briana and Ryan. They were the most stubborn of the family but still, Briana smiled and said in a strong Irish accent, "To keel Lilith, I'd do anythin'. Of course, we will fight next to ya."

Elizabeth put her hand to her chest as she looked at them terrified. Not only had they arrived, but more would come to assist. She closed her eyes and looked around the room wondering who would survive. Tears blurred her vision as she realized that no matter how much she hoped and no matter how much she prayed, the war had officially started. She swallowed hard knowing that soon blood *would* spill.

Chapter Fourteen
Safety Reigns

Lilith smiled softly as she stood within the living room of Bernard's house. She looked around and sighed happily as she thought of her plan. Nothing had been ruined by Bridget's escape. She would still gain Marissa's fortune.

Her head tilted as she heard him enter. Marissa's scent swirled around him as he walked into the room. She turned to face him.

"You've been with Marissa," she said with a secret smile

on her face.

"How else do you expect me to gain her trust?" He asked, angrily as he walked further into the room.

"And do you have it?" She asked stepping closer. Her smile was wide as she purred, "Do you have her trust?"

He looked at her guarded. Something was wrong with the way she looked at him, "I do."

She raised her eye brows as she stepped closer and caressed his face, "And you do want me happy, don't you?"

He narrowed his eyes, "Regardless of whether I want you happy or not, I have to make you happy."

She gave a short laugh, "How right you are."

Bernard rolled his eyes and let out an exasperated sigh, "Are we done with this conversation? I need to feed and I need some rest."

Her smile widened as her purr deepened, "No, we are not done with this conversation."

"What else do you want to discuss?" He asked, annoyed.

"Marissa," she said and then, stepped closer to him, "Since you have her trust, it is time to take the next step. I'm getting bored with the courtship."

Bernard turned to her abruptly. His heart jumped in his chest, "What are you talking about?"

"It's time for you to kill her," she said, matter of factly. She stepped in front of him, "It's time for you to get rid of the last of your humanity."

Bernard swallowed as a tremble shook him. He knew better than to argue, "When do you want it done?"

She smiled, "Tomorrow night," she said with a laugh, "I want to begin her family's destruction soon and hers sooner."

Bernard forced the next words out of his mouth, "Okay,

Mother."

She patted his cheek and then, left the room. He closed his eyes, knowing that he was out of time and so was Marissa.

****

Seth heard Miss Kimela before he knew what had happened. She had backed into his room, tears stood in her eyes and he could tell that many more had fallen. Seth blinked in the darkness, seeing that she held something. He squinted harder trying to make out the shape. When he finally did, he was surprised to see that she was holding a shotgun. His eyes widened knowing that they were in danger.

Quickly, he went to the bed that Bridget lay upon and pulled her to him. He knew that there was no time to escape and all that he could do was try to comfort Bridget who was already crying in the darkness.

"You have to get her quiet, Darling," Miss Kimela said, "Otherwise, we'll all be dead."

Seth realized that Miss Kimela was trying in vain. He understood that the vampires had come. Still, he wouldn't upset Miss Kimela further.

"Do you hear that, Bridget?" Seth whispered to her and the little girl nodded her head quieting nearly instantaneously.

Seth watched Miss Kimela, studying her in the dark. That's when he saw them. Two scarlet strands ran from what Seth recognized as vampire bites. A tremble shook him as he realized that he had not been safe at all and he had put everyone who had helped him in danger.

Seth's mouth went dry as the door burst in. Two shots from the rifle did nothing to deter the vampires at the door. Seth closed his eyes knowing that their fates were sealed.

"Demons!" Miss Kimela screamed, making Seth open his

eyes wide.

Then, Seth saw them. They were Bart and Reginald, the two vampires that had guarded Bridget. Bart, the biggest laughed at Miss Kimela.

"Demons, huh?" He asked with a grin on his face, "This comes from a whore."

He bit his wrist and pushed it to her mouth, forcing her to drink the blood that poured from it, "Now, you're a demon whore," he laughed.

A whimper escaped from Bridget's lips and Seth hugged her closer. Bart turned to them, "And you," he said, "You will suffer a far worse fate."

He stalked toward them but stopped as two vampires that Seth had never met before came through the door. One was largely muscled with blonde hair and the other one had nearly black hair and seemed a bit boyish.

They looked toward Seth and then Bart. It seemed to Seth that the blonde headed vampire disappeared but a second later, he had spun Bart around by the shoulder, planting his fist in his stomach. Bart doubled over and a second later, the vampire had Bart by the throat.

Seth blinked surprised and then, looked toward the door but the dark haired vampire was gone. Seth looked around the room and finally found him holding Reginald off of the ground by his shirt.

"Close your eyes," the blonde vampire said and Seth realized what he was going to do. He covered Bridget's eyes protectively but kept his open. When the blonde vampire was sure that Bridget wasn't looking, he gave a brutal twist to Bart's head and suddenly it was detached from his body, instantly turning the vampire to ash.

164.

Seth heard a short scream from Reginald and he was no more. Slowly, Seth looked up at the unknown vampires. He didn't know whether to be terrified or relieved because they could still be Lilith's followers. She could have wanted Reginald and Bart dead for allowing them to escape.

Seth slowly raised his eyes to the blonde vampire but he wasn't looking at Seth but at Bridget. Seth hugged her closer to his chest. Finally, the vampire looked at him and managed a smile.

"I am Ares," the blonde headed vampire said stepping forward, "And my friend is Dominic. Don't be frightened. We won't harm you."

Seth looked from Ares to Dominic, confused. Dominic put up his hands, "I know that you must be frightened, but it seems that this lady needs my assistance. I see that she was bitten but did they change her?"

Seth nodded his head once at him, "Bart changed her," Seth said.

"Do you know her name?" Dominic asked, kneeling next to Miss Kimela's shivering body on the floor.

"Miss Kimela," Seth replied, distressed, "She helped us. She let us stay here."

Ares looked at the shivering woman with a worried glance, "I promise that she'll be well taken care of," he said, softly, "She will suffer no more for the kindness that she's given."

Ares slowly turned back to Seth, "I owe you for everything that you've done for Bridget," he said, "I know that you don't understand that but I'll explain it as simply as I can. Bernard is my son. Bridget is my granddaughter."

Bridget raised her head at the mention of her father's name, "I want my Daddy and momma," she said in her little angel's voice.

"And I will take you to them," he said and then looked at Seth, "Caben, do you have anywhere to go? Do you have family?"

"My name isn't Caben. Only Lilith called me that," Seth said, softly, "It's Seth. And no. I don't have anywhere to go. I don't have any family."

"Then, you'll stay with us," Ares said, smiling.

Seth looked at Ares and then Dominic warily. Ares stepped toward Seth and frowned, "We need to get you all out of here," he said, "I am positive that others will follow them. I don't want you or Bridget to be harmed when they do."

Seth looked toward Miss Kimela, "What about her?" He asked, frowning.

"We're taking her with us," he said and frowned, "Dominic, we'll need a place for her to stay. She can't be around them…the bloodlust."

"I know some vampires near Winchester that will take her in until it has passed," he said and then looked at Seth, "I promise you that she'll be safe."

Seth shook his head and rose from the bed. He reached to pick Bridget up but she bounded off of the bed grabbing not only his hand but shyly grasping Ares'. Seth tensed and when the vampire didn't attack, he went limp with relief. He closed his eyes realizing that they were safe at last.

****

Marissa stared out at the darkening sky, feeling her heart in her throat. Something didn't feel right. Something ominous was about to happen. It was thick in the air. Nicolas stood near her and he frowned as he touched her cheek.

"Is everything okay?" He asked, frowning as he gazed

166.

down at her.

"Yes," she whispered as she peered up at him.

He frowned as he studied her face, "For some reason, I don't believe you."

"Honestly, I'm just tired," she said and then, sighed, "All of this worry has caused me to expect the worst. I simply need sleep."

He hugged her, "Well, don't worry," he said, kissing her softly, "I won't let anything bad happen."

"I know," she said, wrapping her arms around him.

"However, I do have to leave now," he said with a sigh, "The families are here and there is a lot I have to discuss with him."

"I understand," she said, smiling as she caressed his cheek.

"Just call for me if you need me," he said, giving her a crooked grin, "All you have to do is say my name and I'll be here."

She nodded and he kissed her forehead. Then, he was gone. She stood on her balcony for a long moment. When she turned to go inside she was confronted with Bernard. She studied him and then, frowned. She understood even before he told her that her time had come. Lilith had ordered her death.

"It's okay, Bernard," she whispered, "I know why you are here."

A tear fell down his cheek as he faced her, "She wants it done tomorrow night."

Marissa nodded, "I don't think I should tell Nicolas. He'll only try to stop you."

"I wish there was a way to stop me," he whispered, stepping close to her, "I don't want to hurt you."

"I know you don't," she said, looking up into his eyes, "But I understand."

"I'll make it as painless as I can," he said as a sob ripped from his throat.

Slowly, she wrapped her arms around him and allowed him to sob as her hopes to save her mortality vanished.

Chapter Fifteen
Mortality

Seth looked at Miss Kimela as the truck that Ares and Dominic had procured rambled along down a road in a town an hour from Winchester, Tennessee. It was a road which was all but unused. Images of the blood shed at the brothel flashed through his mind, making him shiver.

Only two other people had survived. One was the trucker, Charles Ostens, and the other had been the pretty girl that had called to him, Nora Lynch. Both sat wide eyed in the cab of the truck, cautiously looking at Miss Kimela who lay in the bed of the truck in middle of her transition. Tears had stained Nora's pretty cheeks and blood coated her neck. Charles had been bitten but faired much better than Nora.

Dominic looked at them and sighed heavily as he pulled the truck to the side of the road, "We have to figure out what to do about you two," he mumbled and both of them looked up at him frightened.

Dominic turned to face them. His usual good humor was gone as he looked at Charles first.

"I'm not going to hurt you," he said and then, bit his lip, "But I'm worried that you've been drained too far and you will die if something is not done very soon."

Charles nodded his head weakly and Nora began to sob, "I don't want to die!"

Dominic looked down the street, ignoring her outbursts, "In a few moments, we will reach the town where another family of vampires live. They will be taking care of Miss Kimela. They can take care of you too."

"Until we die?" Charles whispered, looking up at Dominic, fearfully.

"Either that or until you've gone through the change," he said and then, looked at him pointedly, "Then, you will be part of their family and ours."

"There's a way that we won't die?" Charles asked, nearly desperate.

"There is," Dominic said, raising his brow, "you will never die if you choose this option. You will live forever. You will always look as you do now. You won't age. However, you will crave the blood of living creatures. You will be a vampire. You will have a difficult time at first. It will be torturous. However, my family will keep you from harming humans while you go through the worst parts of the change. Now, all that you have to do is choose."

"I choose to be a vampire!" Nora said, nearly as soon as he had said the words.

Dominic looked at the girl with an intensity in his eyes that frightened Seth, "Do you understand that it is painful?"

"Yes," Nora said as tears fell down her cheeks.

"Do you understand that you won't be human anymore?" He asked, frowning.

Nora raised her chin, "I'm a whore, Sir," she said, sniffling, "I haven't been treated well as a person anyway. Still, I'd prefer to live even if it is the way you described. So, yes, I do understand everything."

Dominic looked at Charles and he nodded his head, "I choose to live too."

Dominic closed his eyes disappointed. When he opened his eyes he looked at Ares, seeing a grim look upon his face. They never liked to change anyone. Still, they had given them a choice. They had done everything that they could do.

"Do you have ta bite me again?" Nora asked with wide eyes.

"No," Dominic answered in a quiet voice, "You've been drained enough," she looked confused so he continued, "You'll have to drink from me."

She shook her head. Slowly, Dominic lowered her beside Miss Kimela. Nora was trembling.

"It's alright, Nora," he said, gently, "You won't hurt yet. It's when the change happens that you will. The hunger hurts."

She shook her head, looking up as Charles lay next to her. It warmed Dominic's heart to see that they clasped each other's hands.

Dominic sighed as he pulled his knife from his jeans pocket. He slit his hand, making sure that the blood flowed freely before handing it to Ares for him to do the same. Dominic pressed his hand to Nora's lips and slowly, she began to drink.

He felt each gentle pull of her lips. His blood flowed into her mouth, leaving him tingling and thirsty all at once. He felt his teeth grow and tears burned his eyes as he felt the painful need burning through him.

He pulled away from her, swallowing hard. He didn't look at Seth or Bridget. He couldn't. During this moment, it was too hard to resist harming them.

Instead, he spoke to Seth in what sounded like a growl, "Watch them."

He bounded out of the truck bed and ran into the woods, searching for an animal that would calm his thirst. He could hear Ares following him into the forest.

Dominic doubled over in pain. He forced himself to sense what was near. Finally, he sensed what he needed.

Come to me, he commanded the creature.

A few moments later, a deer stood before him. It was magnificent with large antlers rising from it's head. He didn't study it any further. He wasn't interested in it's beauty. Instead, he became the predator that he was and he fed on the deer's blood.

****

Aphrodite closed her eyes listening to the sound of her husband's voice. Tears rested in her eyes at the relief of the message. He had retrieved Bridget and he had also saved a boy named Seth. They would be in Winchester within the hour. She looked up at the darkening sky and smiled as she focused on her son.

172.

A frown crossed her brow as she entered his mind. The only thing she saw was his conversation with Lilith. He was being forced to change Marissa that very night. She felt his hopelessness. She felt his heartache. Panic entered her heart as she tried to reach his mind but he blocked her. He had blocked everyone.

She closed her eyes and sent what she saw in Bernard's mind to Ares, begging him to hurry and then, she went in search of Bernard in hopes that she could stop him from making the worst mistake of his long life.

Chapter Sixteen
Homecomings

The significance of life is that all creatures have both good and evil within them. As Marissa Dalene looked into the eyes of the creature that approached her, she saw all of the contrasts of that belief. He was both man and monster…friend and enemy and someone who she both loved and hated.

She watched his gait trying to decide whether it was predatory or not as he came closer and closer. Her heart sped up;

pounding the blood through her veins in what seemed a last attempt to stay alive.

She closed her eyes and swallowed over the lump in her throat as her name whispered softly to her on the breeze. Slowly, she took a deep breath and looked up into the eyes of the one who would choose her fate.

"Marissa," he said, again and tears rested in his eyes. It was another contrast. He felt guilt for the evil deeds he had done and would still do. She swallowed as she realized that if he suffered from guilt, her fate was sealed.

Her lips trembled as a single tear fell from her eye as he reached for her in silence. He said nothing. He offered no apology. She didn't move away but sighed as he pulled her to him. She closed her eyes against the darkness as he lowered his head to her throat causing another tear to fall down her cheek. However, this tear was in mourning because she faced her death.

She could feel the points of his teeth begin to break the skin. She inhaled with the pain as the tips began to pierce flesh. A drop of blood fell down her shoulder as the first layer of skin was broken.

"Stop!" She heard a woman's voice scream just as he began to bite harder. He pulled away and Marissa touched her neck. Only a drop of blood had been spilled. Slowly, she looked up to find a beautiful woman with long blonde hair. Her eyes were the same shocking blue as Bernard's.

She stepped toward him, "Don't hurt her!" She screamed still too far away to be heard clearly. Still, she ran until she stood in front of him, "You don't have to hurt her."

"What about Bridget?" He asked, terrified.

"Ares has her," she said, smiling, "A boy that lived there, saved her from Lilith. He found out that she was going to change her. His name is Seth. He's also with them. He says he knows you."

"Is that Thalia's son?" Marissa asked with wide eyes.

"Yes," he said, breathing a sigh of relief.

"So, does that mean that I'm safe?" She asked, smiling.

He nodded, "From me, you are," he said, "We'll still have to protect you from Lilith but she can't force me to do anything anymore."

Marissa smiled as she heard a little girl's voice, "Daddy!" She yelled. Marissa's eyes widened as she saw the little girl throw herself into his arms. Tears flowed down his face as he hugged her. He looked up at the boy who was with her.

"Thank you, Seth," he said, softly, "Thank you."

Marissa's mouth dropped open as she studied the boy before her. She swallowed as she stared at the similarites he had with Thalia. Slowly, she turned back to Bernard.

"Thalia needs to know her son is here," Marissa said, softly, "She needs to have him back. She's waited too long."

Seth turned to her obviously in shock as he took in what she said, "My mother lives here?"

"Yes, your mother lives here but also your father, your brother and your sister," she said, smiling as she took his hand. Your mother has cried for you. Your family wants to meet you. Do you want to meet them?"

His eyes filled with tears as he nodded his head, "I do. I want to meet them."

Marissa looked at Bernard, "I'll take him to them."

Bernard smiled, "The boy deserves to have his mother. Thank you, Seth."

Seth nodded as he went to Bridget and hugged her, "Be a good girl," he whispered and then, kissed her head, "I'll see you

176.
soon."

Bridget nodded as she moved from her father's arms to throw her arms around Seth's waist, "I love you, Seth."

"I love you too, Bridget," he said and then, he moved away.

A blonde headed man stepped forward and Marissa stared at him, knowing that he was a vampire, "I'm Bernard's father, Ares," he said, smiling, "I think it's still a bit too soon for you to walk around at night by yourself. Lilith is still out there and my son is busy so, I think I should escort you and the boy."

Marissa nodded, "Thank you," and then, she turned to Seth, "Are you ready to meet your family."

He smiled, "I'm more than ready."

****

Thalia heard the knock on her door and frowned. It was almost midnight. No one had ever visited her that late. William looked up from his book into her face. Fear was clearly marked there.

Slowly, she rose and went to the door with William behind her. She looked out of the window instantly feeling relief. She looked back at William and nodded to tell him it was alright.

"It's Marissa. What is she doing here so late?" She asked as she unlocked the door. William shrugged but did not move from his position behind her. .

She pulled the door open and faced Marissa, "Is everything alright?" She asked, concerned, "No one is hurt, are they?"

Marissa smiled, "Everything is more than alright," she said, beaming "I'm actually here to introduce you to someone…Though you've already met him."

She stepped to the side and allowed Seth to walk to the

door. Thalia's eyes widened as she took in his appearance. She saw her pigment of caramel in his skin and copper and black hair. Slowly, her eyes met his finding the same shade of eyes as her own. A cry stuck in her throat as her hand flew to her chest.

William gasped, "Is that Seth?"

Thalia nodded as tears fell down her cheeks. She stepped forward and looked into his eyes, "Yes, it is," she said, "Seth has come home."

Seth closed his eyes as she reached forward to caress his cheek, "I thought you had died," She whispered and then, she hugged him. Slowly, he wrapped his arms around his mother and began to sob.

Marissa smiled as she backed away allowing Thalia to bring her son into her home and into her life. She smiled as she realized that everything was finally over. There was only one person who she needed to tell…Nicolas.

****

Nicolas heard Marissa's call to him as soon as she whispered his name. In an instant, he was racing through the forest which separated their properties, only stopping when he came to a familiar scent. Automatically, he searched for its source.

Finally, his eyes rested upon Bernard, standing ten feet away from him. He frowned as every muscle in his body tensed, "What are you doing here?" He asked, studying Bernard's face.

"I'm not here to fight with you, if that's what you think," he said, rolling his eyes, "I came to speak with you about Marissa."

Nicolas took a step toward him, "What about her?" He asked, angrily, "Have you hurt her?"

Bernard pursed his lips, "You really do think the worst of

me."

"What do you expect, Bernard?" He asked as his nostrils flared, "You've done nothing but harm my family."

Bernard nodded his head, "And I intend to rectify that," he said, and then, sighed heavily, "I want you to know that though the night could have ended differently, Marissa is unharmed and human. My daughter has been returned and Thalia also has her son. Of course, Marissa would have told you that when you saw her."

"Then, why the personal visit?" He asked, suspicious.

"Because I want to make something clear to you," he said, stepping closer.

"What is that, Bernard?" He asked, studying his face.

"I want you to know that I care about Marissa," he said, looking into Nicolas' eyes, "She is my only friend. If I can ever do anything for her, I will do it. I want you to know that."

Nicolas tilted his head, surprised, "I'll keep that in mind."

"One more thing and then, I will let you go to her," he said, shifting uncomfortably, "The one thing I regret doing that I wasn't forced to do was attacking you and your family. I don't expect you to accept it but I do apologize."

Nicolas nodded, "Is that all?"

"That's all," he said and then, he was gone, leaving Nicolas confused but oddly freed.

****

Nicolas found Marissa on her balcony. Her hair whipped behind her in the wind. He couldn't help but to watch her while she was oblivious to him. Her face was turned up to the night in complete peace. Her eyes searched the lawn below.

"If you are going to keep company with vampires, you should know that we can appear anywhere," he said, causing her to whip around to face him.

"Nicolas," she said, grinning widely as she stood in front of him.

He reached forward and caressed her face, "Promise me that you'll be more careful."

She tilted her head as she stared into his eyes, "I will. Besides, there is less to worry about now."

"I've heard," he said, pulling her to him.

She allowed him to press his lips to hers before she pulled back, "How did you find out?"

"I spoke to Bernard," he said, nuzzling her neck with his nose. He could feel her tense beneath him.

"You were nice, weren't you?" She asked, alarmed.

He kissed along her jaw, "If you're asking if I harmed, maimed or killed him, the answer is no."

She relaxed, "Good," she breathed.

He pulled away from her to look into her eyes, "You care about him?" He asked, frowning.

She shrugged, "He's my friend."

"He was going to kill you," he said, frowning.

"He would have found a way not to," she said, giving a small smile, "He was trying to save his daughter."

"Well, it should make you happy to know that he told me you were his only friend and he cares about you," he said, "I still don't trust him but I know you'd want to know."

"Well, now that everything is over, I hope this horrible feud between you two can end," she said and then, raised her brow, "After all, if you hadn't been changed, you wouldn't have met me and plus, your original feaud over Giselle doesn't matter anymore since you have no interest in her."

He sighed, "It will still be a while before Bernard and

180.
Giselle are welcomed into my family," he said, caressing her cheek, "But I will tolerate them for you."

She smiled, "See doesn't that make your heart a little lighter."

He shook his head, "No," he said, "But you do."

She smiled as he kissed her feeling happier than she had ever been.

Epilogue

Nicolas smiled as he looked up at the Dalene house. Marissa had just left him and for the first time, he could breathe a sigh of relief. She was safe and he didn't have to worry anymore. He took one last look and then, turned to leave.

He had taken a couple of steps before he saw movement from the corner of his eye. He blinked in surprise. finding Abigail standing in the moonlight. Slowly, he walked to her, stopping just in front of her. She glanced over his shoulder, glancing at the Dalene's house before looking back into his face.

"How's Marissa?" She asked in a voice that was oddly

strained.

He tilted his head, studying her. She seemed tense, "She's fine," he said, suddenly cautious, "She's happy that everything is over."

Abigail looked past him at the Dalene's house again. A frown marked her face. Nicolas felt his stomach began to twist. Something was wrong.

"Are the leaders of the families returning home?" He asked, still studying her face.

Finally, she faced him. The look on her face caused his heart to nearly skid to a stop. Slowly, she shook her head, "No, they won't be returning," she said, looking nearly grief-stricken, "The others will be coming soon."

"But Marissa isn't going to be turned," he said, suddenly panicked, "Bernard isn't going to do it."

"Maybe not," she said with a shrug, "But she will change."

Nicolas closed his eyes as tears came to his eyes, "She can't become one of us," he said, shaking his head. Then, he looked into her eyes, "I don't want this life for her."

Abigail smiled sadly, "It doesn't matter what you want, Nick," she whispered, softly, "She's destined to be one of us. She's destined for more than that."

"What could she be destined for that is so important?" Nicolas asked angrily.

Abigail looked at the Dalene's house once more before looking back at Nicolas, "There's a reason why she draws all of our attention," she said and then, smiled, "She's destined to bring us out of the darkness."

Nicolas shook his head, "And how would she do that?"

Abigail smiled, "Don't you know?" She asked and when

Nicolas did not answer, her smile widened, "She's going to kill Lilith."

The Hidden (Book 1) The Alexandra Denton Chronicles

New Cover!!
The Hidden (Book 1) The Alexandra
Denton Chronicle
Available in most e-book formats. Also,
Available in paperback!!

The Appointed (Book 2) The Alexandra Denton Chronicles

New Cover coming in October 2014!!
Available in Kindle, Nook and Paperback!
Will be available in more e-book formats in October!!

The Fallen (Book 3) The Alexandra Denton Chronicles

The Fallen
The Alexandra Denton Chronicles

Amanda K. Dudley-Penn

Available on Kindle!!
Coming in April to Nook!!

The Sacrifice (Book 4) The Alexandra Denton Chronicles

Coming in December 2014 to Kindle!!

Beckoned (Book 1) The Brazil Werewolf Series

Original cover   New Cover

New Cover coming in June!!

Available in Kindle, Nook and
paperback!
   Will be available in most e-book
         formats in June!

Summoned (Book 2) The Brazil Werewolf Series

Available in Kindle and Nook!!
Coming to Paperback in April 2014!!
Enticed (Book 3) The Brazil Werewolf Series

Coming to Kindle in August 2014!!

Unbound (Book 2) The Preston Vampire Series

Coming Soon to Kindle:
April 30, 2014!!

Coming in 2015
The Angel Essence Series!!

Amanda K. Dudley-Penn was born in June 1977 in Tullahoma, Tennessee. She has loved writing from a very young age and spent her time writing stories and poetry for those closest to her. It quickly became her dream to become a published writer. With the support of her husband and children, she began to write her first novel, The Hidden in 2008 and finished it in June of 2012. She is currently the author of three series, The Alexandra Denton Chronicles, The Brazil Werewolf Series and The Preston Vampire Series. She is currently developing a fouth series, The Angel Essence Series. She currently lives in Grand Prairie, Texas with her husband, David and her three children, Constance, Isabella and Joshua.

www.ingramcontent.com/pod-product-compliance
Lightning Source LLC
Chambersburg PA
CBHW070853120626
46556CB00002B/966

* 9 7 8 0 6 1 5 9 6 1 0 9 5 *